A Seductive Arrangement

Dara Girard

ILORI
Press Books, LLC

For Kemi
Rest in peace

Other books by Dara Girard

The Black Stockings Society

Power Play

A Gentleman's Offer

Body Chemistry

Round the Clock

Return of the Black Stockings Society

Playing for Keeps

After Hours

A Private Affair

Just One Look

Private Lessons

Henson Series

Table for Two

Gaining Interest

Careless Rapture

Dangerous Curves

Familiar Stranger

The Clifton Sisters

The Sapphire Pendant

The Amber Stone

The Fortune Brothers

A Tempting Proposal

It Happened One Wedding

Unexpected Pleasure

Midnight Promise

Sweet Temptation

Always and Forever

Novels

Illusive Flame

Honest Betrayal

The Daughters of Winston Barnett

Remember My Name

Chapter One

"Your wife is here."

Jackson Fortune lazily rolled onto his side and squinted up at his personal assistant. The bedroom in his apartment was so bright it felt like a thousand lights had burst into his room all at once, trying their best to sear his pupils.

He closed his eyes with a groan and waved towards the lamp. "Turn that off."

"It is off."

Jackson carefully opened one eye wondering why the room was so bright then realized he hadn't closed the blinds last night. The morning's sun rays ate up every shadow in the room. He feebly gestured to the window, desperate for relief. "You know what to do."

He heard his assistant's steady gait as he walked over to the blinds. "These blinds are the least of your worries. You have a very urgent matter to deal with right now."

Jackson absently rubbed his forehead, wishing his assistant didn't feel the need to use so many words so early in the morning. "Yeah…right. What did you just say?"

The painful sunlight disappeared as he heard the blinds close then his assistant return to the side of his bed. "I said your wife is here."

Jackson blinked waiting for the punch line. Before he could respond, he heard the bed sheets shift next to him and felt a warm, smooth leg brush against his. He turned to his bedmate and blinked. He'd forgotten he hadn't been sleeping alone. She was pretty with light cocoa skin and dark hair that was pleasantly tousled around her head and her name was…

She had a name. Of course she had a name. They always had a name. What was her name?

Her eyes narrowed. Not a good sign. "I didn't know you had a wife."

Jackson blinked quickly, trying to clear his fuzzy brain. Right…a wife. That's why he'd been shaken awake when he'd hoped to sleep in a few more hours. He turned back to his assistant. At least he knew his name. It was Reginald Bowler, but he called him "Bo" because he didn't like the sound of his surname and thought his first name had too many syllables. Bo hadn't worked for him very long. Was it eight months now? The length of his service was about as unremarkable as the man. He wasn't very tall, had a slightly ruddy complexion, tufts of grey hair and serious features. Serious was good.

His previous assistant had disappeared without explanation. Just left a resignation letter on the kitchen countertop without even the decency to at least let the chef know what to prepare for dinner. That had been annoying. The entire reason he had an assistant was to handle the issues he didn't want to. He had better things to do with his time.

Perhaps Bo had a hidden sense of humor and was playing a joke on him. He could take a joke.

Jackson yawned and rubbed his eyes. "I don't," he said, flashing her a smile. "Bo's just teasing."

Reginald cleared his throat and shook his head. "Teasing isn't part of my job description. I left her in the living room."

Jackson became a little more awake. "A woman's really here?"

"Yes."

He sat up. "Saying she's my *wife*?"

Reginald nodded.

"Tell her she has the wrong address."

"I also came to that conclusion, but she's very insistent. She won't leave until you see her."

Jackson slid back under the covers and rested his head on the pillow. "Then make her feel comfortable until she comes to her senses." He was too tired to deal with a crazy woman right now.

"Is that all?"

"Yes."

Jackson heard Reginald's footsteps leave before he closed his eyes. He sighed in frustration when he felt his bedmate nudge him with her foot.

"What?" he mumbled. He just wanted to sleep. It had been a wild night.

"What are you doing?" she asked.

He pulled up the sheet to his chin. "Do I really have to answer that?"

"Aren't you even curious?"

"Curious about what?"

She pulled the sheet down to his waist. "The woman."

Jackson rolled onto his back and looked up at her. Ooh…pretty eyes. Nice breasts. Damn what was her name? "No."

"There's a woman in your living room claiming to be your wife and you can just lie here and try to go back to sleep?"

"You say that as if it were a problem."

"Are you sure you're not married?"

"Of course I'm sure…" He stopped and bit his lip, wishing he could come up with a name. He'd sound more sincere that way. He swore. What was her name? She had a West African look and her accent sounded French. So he knew she was from one of those French speaking countries.

"I'm not sure I believe you." She turned her back to him and swung her legs over the side of the bed. "I'm going." She stood and began to change.

The bed felt cold without her and he hated feeling cold. Did she have a French name? Estelle? Coline? Marie? Probably not. Perhaps if he could remember what country she came from that could give him a clue. Was it Benin? Burundi? Niger?

"You don't have to go yet. It's all a misunderstanding I'm sure. I enjoyed last night." *What I can remember of it.* "And I'd like to see you again. Are you traveling back home to…" He let his words trail off hoping she'd fill in the blanks.

She zipped up her formfitting red dress. "No, I have work in Sweden."

Damn. "I'd like to see you again."

"Take care of your wife first." She stepped into her matching heels.

"I told you I don't have a—"

She grabbed her black clutch from off of his dresser. "*Adieu.*"

He felt the finality in her word. "Don't you mean *Au revoir?*"

"No." She left and closed the door behind her.

Damn and he still didn't know what her name was. Too bad. He pulled the sheets back up and closed his eyes. It didn't work. He couldn't go back to sleep. This stranger, possibly some tipsy ex-girlfriend of his that Bo couldn't identify, had ruined a perfect morning. Jackson kicked the bed sheets off in frustration. He just wanted to sleep.

He wasn't a morning person; he could barely function before ten and it was…

He glanced at his clock and saw it said ten thirty-six. Okay, but it was Saturday and he usually got up after twelve on a weekend. Plus, he'd had a late night. He wasn't like his brother James who would be showered, dressed and have solved the mystery of the confused woman who thought she was his wife by now.

Another couple of minutes and then he'd deal with her. If he was lucky, she'd give up and go home. The thought brought a smile to his face as he reached over, pulled up the sheets and sunk back into his pillow.

An hour later he woke up feeling refreshed. He took a shower, grabbed a robe and headed for the kitchen ready for something to eat.

He walked past the living room and paused when he saw a woman sitting there reading a book. A woman! A woman he didn't recognize because her head was lowered and her long dark hair framed her face, putting it in shadow. He swore. He'd forgotten about her. He dashed into the kitchen before she looked up and spotted him.

He rushed over to Reginald who stood at the sink washing a glass. Jackson gestured to the living room. "Who is that?"

Reginald set the glass on the drying rack before turning to him. "Your wife."

Jackson's brows shot up. "That lunatic is still here?"

"You told me to tell her to wait."

"I was kidding."

"You didn't tell me that."

"I didn't think she'd stay." He rested his hip against the counter. "Did she tell you what she wanted?"

"Only to see you. I told you she was insistent."

Fine. He'd deal with her after he'd eaten. Maybe waiting a little longer may encourage her to leave.

But she was still there after his breakfast of avocado toast with egg. He walked into the living room, annoyed when she sent him a quick disinterested glance before she returned her gaze to the book. He could tell by the colorful imagery it was a graphic novel. She was probably mad at him. Served her right for playing this prank. He sat down in the soft recliner in front of her.

"What do you want?"

She closed the book but didn't lift her head, keeping her face hidden. "You don't remember me, do you?" she said in a low voice.

That voice stirred something deep inside him. It had a sensual, husky edge that made him think of hot wax and black silk sheets.

He looked her up and down. Her voice was more memorable than the rest of her. She did a disservice to the purple mohair velvet sofa which she sat on and the 1920s Persian carpet her heeled boots rested on. She looked like she was dressed for a job interview in a straight black skirt, blue satin blouse and black boots which suited Virginia in the fall. She was pleasantly proportioned with brown skin and clear manicured nails. If he could see more of her face, maybe he'd remember something.

"If you'd look at me that may help."

She lifted her head and tossed her hair over her shoulder. She wore more makeup than a drag queen.

Nope, that didn't help. She seemed a little familiar but something was off. He could pretend, but then she'd know he was lying. "No."

She tossed the book on the oval shaped table with a sigh. He noticed it was a graphic novel he hadn't finished reading yet. "I was afraid of that."

"Are you sure you haven't confused me with someone else?"

"No, Jackson. I know who you are."

She knew his name. Of course she knew his name. She also knew where he lived and the way she said his name felt familiar. Felt good. There was something very familiar about her. Something he couldn't pinpoint. Yes, that voice…and those lips and that body…but it was also unfamiliar too.

He rubbed his forehead. "Lay it out for me. Why did you say we're married?"

"Because we are. We got married in Las Vegas."

She held up her hand and flashed the ring on her finger. "Don't worry, I only just put it on to show you. I haven't worn it since that night."

That night. Suddenly, it all came flooding back to him. Sort of. He remembered the threat of tears (hers not his). A lot of liquor (definitely him). A limo ride and not much else.

"When?"

"Two months ago."

He stared at her, stunned. "Two months ago and you're just telling me now?"

"Yes, well the thing is…"

Two months ago. He couldn't believe it. Wow. Okay, he had to think. Two months ago…hmm…two months…two months. Two months ago he remembered waking up alone in a hotel room in Las Vegas and catching a flight back to Kirkland before his stepfather gave him the riot act for missing a scheduled meeting. He did remember taking a ring off his finger and briefly feeling victorious for some reason, but it had been a crazy weekend and he was ready to go home so he hadn't thought much of it.

"If we really did get married, why didn't you stay around and—"

"That's what I was trying to explain, if you were listening."

"I wasn't. Sorry. Start over. Why didn't you stay the next morning?"

"That was not part of the deal."

"Deal? You're sure you married me?"

She showed him the papers.

He briefly scanned them then nodded. "Clearly we both made a mistake. What do you want? An annulment? That's fine with me. I'll squash this before anyone finds out."

She bit her lip. "Might be too late for that. I came to apologize. I didn't know who you were—are, and—"

Warning bells rang in his mind. She seemed nice and harmless, but he had to be careful. His tone sharpened. "You want money?"

"No."

"Blackmail?"

"No," she said losing patience. "I will explain everything but first you should change."

"Change?"

"Get yourself together."

"I am together."

She gestured towards him. "You always go around in just your robe?"

He glanced down amused. "Yes." He smiled at her. "Don't worry you're not going to see anything you shouldn't. Now start talking."

"What do you remember?"

He leaned back and rested his arm along the back of the couch. "Clearly not enough."

"I am really sorry about this. I thought I should get to you before someone else does. It was a mistake. I should have erased the pictures from my cell phone. I am willing to get a quick annulment and disappear from your life. At least

I would have done that. I didn't expect my sister to see the pictures of us and then—"

Jackson shook his head. "Hold on. You're not making any sense. Who would get to me?"

"You haven't gotten any calls?"

"No."

"How about—?"

The sound of the doorbell stopped her words.

Jackson stood. "I wonder who that is?"

She sent him a wary look. "Trouble."

Chapter Two

For a moment Toyin thought she was hallucinating. First there was one Jackson and now there were two. Except the man on the other side of the door seemed meaner and darker somehow. They both had the same tall, powerful physique; elegant, clean shaven features and smooth brown skin. But the other man wore a black sports jacket, somber colored grey shirt and trousers—a direct contrast to Jackson's stripped red and yellow robe.

"What have you gotten yourself into?" the man said then stopped when he saw her. "I'm sorry. I didn't realize it was true."

"What's true?" Jackson asked.

The man held out his hand to her. "I'm James Fortune by the way."

"Toyin. Toyin um…" Dear God she'd forgotten her last name. Why did this guy scare her? She already knew she was in trouble but the presence of this man made it all feel worse. "Jacobs."

He gestured to the sofa. "How long have you known my brother?"

She sat down, although she felt like running. "Not long."

"I see." He sat down beside her and turned to Jackson. "When were you going to tell us about her?"

"There's nothing to tell," Jackson said with a shrug. "I hardly know her."

James motioned to Jackson's robe. "You always entertain strangers like that?"

"I was with someone else when she just showed up out of the blue and—"

James surged to his feet. "You did what?"

"I didn't expect her to come."

James turned to her with regret. "I apologize on behalf of—"

"No, it's okay," Toyin said quickly, waving her hands. "It's my fault. I surprised him."

"He surprised all of us."

"It wasn't like that," Jackson said. "I wasn't cheating on her. I—"

James offered her a small smile of regret. "Will you excuse us for a minute?"

Toyin nodded, knowing it wasn't a question. She watched him take his brother's arm, lead him into another room and close the door.

"Would you like anything more to drink?" the ruddy faced man who'd told her to call him Reginald asked her.

"No, thank you."

"They may be a while."

"I should have just told him the truth an hour ago."

"This serves him right," Reginald said with a sly smile. "He shouldn't have kept you waiting."

"I'm sure it wasn't on purpose."

He sent her a look. "Jackson doesn't like to confront things."

"I can't blame him. At least about this. No one was supposed to know about it. It was just a stupid lark. But I'll find a way to fix it."

"You're not the only trouble he's gotten into so don't be too hard on yourself."

Reginald was being kind but she still felt guilty. If her nosy sister hadn't gotten hold of her cell phone her secret would have been safe. A reckless, crazy secret no one was supposed to know about. Something she'd even forgotten about until her sister stopped by her apartment to cheer her up.

"When's the last time you've left this place?" Maryam had asked her yesterday morning as she opened the closed blinds of Toyin's apartment, dust particles dancing all around her. She waved them away then brushed off her tailored white top and green trousers. Her hair was perfectly set in a pixie cut that complimented her oval shaped, earth brown face and small frame.

Toyin lay on her stomach on the couch dressed in a pair of old jeans and a pale blue sweatshirt. She stared at the TV feeling like a beached whale in comparison. She'd lived on the couch the past week. Unwashed dishes sat in the sink and clothes littered the ground along with two empty pizza boxes. She wouldn't cry but she had the right to fall apart. She'd returned from Las Vegas and discovered that the woman she'd hired to run TJ Studios, her web development and animation company, had lied about everything. She'd lied about the distribution opportunities she'd secured, the authors and illustrators she'd hired, the future business opportunities had been a mirage; she'd let contracts slide, and now Toyin was in deep financial trouble. She'd misled her for months!

Toyin had thought the dip in business had been due to competitors not from her manager siphoning off clients and then starting her own rival business. For the past two months she'd been scrambling to recover, but had stopped trying.

Toyin felt on the verge of a nervous breakdown, but she wouldn't cry about it.

"We're worried about you," Maryam said, pushing aside three Chinese and Italian takeaway cartons from the coffee table. "I realize that what happened with TJ Studios is hurtful—"

Toyin pushed up her glasses and glared at her. "Hurtful? You call an employee stealing your clients and designs *hurtful?*"

"Okay, a big betrayal, but you can fight this."

"I'm running out of funds." *And energy and the will to go on.*

"You still have your store to run."

It was small comfort. New Worlds, her comic and pop-culture shop, paid the bills and was something she enjoyed. It was female focused; designed for women to feel comfortable in. A contrast to more known places that had a grimy, leechy, male dominated energy. At New Worlds, women could ask questions without fear of condescension, where as in the larger comic world a woman without an encyclopedic knowledge of the industry is sometimes treated like a pathetic outsider.

With its clean, airy atmosphere, bright colors and knowledgeable friendly staff, New Worlds, had become popular and profitable with a robust online presence that helped maintain their visibility worldwide.

But TJ Studios, which she had set up in the space above the store, had been her passion and now it was over. She had no new projects and no energy to develop them or seek out new clients. "I have a manager who runs the store. I don't need to be there."

Maryam looked around the apartment in dismay, briefly scrunching her face at the sight of a large poster of Wonder Woman and another of Storm from X-Men. "This isn't like you. You can't live like this. It isn't healthy."

"I don't care." She didn't care much about anything since Shanna's deception and she didn't even want to think about Lance...

"Where's your cell phone?"

Toyin pulled her phone out of her back pocket and handed it to her. "Why?"

"I need to find someone you can talk to."

She groaned. Maryam could be irritating. An electrical engineer by trade and a pain in the ass by nature, her sister didn't know when to give up. "I'm talking to you, aren't I?"

"You need someone else to help you out of this funk."

"I don't want to talk to anyone. That's the point." Toyin motioned to the door. "Now go away."

Maryam searched through Toyin's cell phone. "It's amazing how many pictures you have on this thing. Do you even remember them all?"

Toyin sighed and pointed to the door. "If you're going to judge me, go home."

Maryam gasped and paused. "Who is this?"

"I don't know," Toyin said with little interest as she grabbed her TV remote to search for another show to binge watch. Preferably something with more than fifty episodes. She didn't want to think.

Maryam enlarged the image and peered closer. "You have to know."

Something in her sister's tone told Toyin something bad was about to happen. She reached for the cell phone. "Let me see."

"Who is this man?" Maryam said, holding up the phone so Toyin could see the screen, but keeping it out of reach.

Toyin's heart constricted in horror as she stared at Jackson's face. She'd forgotten all about him and Las Vegas. "He's nobody," Toyin said, hoping her calm voice didn't make her sister suspicious. She returned her gaze to the TV hoping to look disinterested, her mouth suddenly dry. "I'll talk to Tansy later so you don't need to worry."

Maryam continued to look at the photos. "You did a great job with Photoshop."

Toyin closed her eyes wishing she hadn't taken so many pictures with him. "Yes, Photoshop is amazing."

"Except I don't think you would have manipulated so many pictures unless you had a strange obsession with this guy since you and Lance broke up."

"Right."

"Tell me the truth. Are these pictures real?"

Toyin hesitated.

"Don't tell me these pictures are real."

Toyin decided to be defensive. If she was defensive her sister may apologize and change the subject. It was the only tactic she could think of. She sat up and folded her arms. "Why wouldn't they be real?"

Her sister sent her a long, considering look and Toyin quickly realized she'd used the wrong strategy. Maryam had a more devious mind than she did. Because Maryam had chosen the more traditional route in life—graduate degree in engineering like their parents, marriage and children—no one in the family knew that on her study abroad in Belgium she'd had two lovers; she sometimes shoplifted small items and had a tattoo on her right inner thigh. She'd championed Toyin's career choice and finally helped their parents see some merit in her career as a cartoonist, illustrator and store owner.

"You don't know who this is," she said with a knowing grin.

"Of course I do," Toyin said, now feeling defensive for real. "You're the one who asked me."

"Because I was surprised to see him on your phone."

"It's nothing. He's just some guy I met in Las Vegas."

Maryam narrowed her eyes. "You're not telling me something."

Toyin held out her hand, motioning to the cell phone. "Did you find what you were looking for?"

Maryam held the cell phone close, her eyes wide with interest. "What happened?"

Toyin cleared her throat, folded her arms and glanced down; pushing an empty soda can aside with her foot. "Nothing."

"Then why are you two in front of a chapel?"

She shrugged, gripping her arms tighter. "The chapel was just there."

Maryam leaned forward and lowered her voice. "What did you do?"

Toyin met her sister's eyes then sighed in defeat. She could never stand up to her sister's lethal stare. That piercing look always made her feel as if she were five-years-old on the verge of being grounded. "I got married."

Maryam fell back in her seat as if dodging a punch. "You did *what?*"

Toyin threw out her hands. "I was depressed. He came along and cheered me up. We both had too much to drink and thought…*Screw the world let's do something crazy* and we did. I haven't gotten around to contacting him and fixing things because I got home and—"

"You got married?"

"Yes."

Maryam pointed to the photo, her hand shaking. "To him?"

Toyin sighed and nodded. "But you can't tell Mum and Dad."

Maryam waved the cell phone. "Are you *sure* you married this guy?"

Toyin rolled her eyes. "Why do you keep asking me that? Yes. I'm sure. Positive. One hundred percent." She snatched the cell phone and showed another image of Jackson kissing her on the cheek. "See? This is not something I could make up." She thought of a comic she'd created about a woman who could talk to the dead with a ninja squirrel as her sidekick. Her family knew she had a wild imagination. "Okay, scratch that, I could make it up, but I didn't."

"You're amazing."

Toyin tossed the cell phone on the table and lay back down. "I know."

"You don't know who he is."

Toyin growled in frustration. Why wouldn't her sister listen? "Yes, I do. His name is Jackson Fortune."

Maryam shook her head. "No, who he *really* is."

Toyin frowned. "He's not Jackson Fortune?"

"Yes, but he's more than just a name. This is why I've told you to read the business section and the articles I forward to you. How you can expect to run a lucrative business and not do so is beyond me."

Toyin stuck out her tongue.

"Does his family know about you?" Maryam asked.

"No, nobody knows about this. What are you doing?" she asked when her sister picked up her phone and started typing.

"I'm going to help you."

She sat up and reached for the cell phone. "I don't need your help."

Maryam moved the cell phone out of reach and continued typing. "Yes, you do. You've got a golden ticket and you don't even know it. Fortunately, I do. This is what big sisters are for."

Toyin stood up to grab it. "Maryam—"

Maryam jumped out of her seat and backed away, her gaze never leaving the screen. "You leave this to me. You need money and he's loaded."

"Wait. No!" Toyin grabbed her sister's arm. "He helped me out already and—"

Maryam pushed "Send" with her free thumb then handed the cell phone to Toyin with a big smile. "That's the problem with you. You're too nice. Opportunities like this don't come every day."

Toyin stared down at her cell phone horrified. "What have you done?"

"Changed your life."

For better or worse? Toyin now wondered as she looked around Jackson's stylish bachelor pad, her gaze spotting an original Basquiat painting and vintage French coffee tables. She buried her face in her hands. Her life had changed enough as it was. She didn't need any more change.

How was she supposed to know that the drunken stranger she'd married was the stepson of the founder of BioMed Solutions? A multi-million dollar company. How could she have imagined that her bossy sister had been able to create a major social media storm with a few choice words and interesting pictures? Weren't most things posted online ignored? Weren't millions of things posted every day? How could this stupid story have gained any traction?

But it had and that was why she had to warn Jackson because Maryam's action hadn't only changed her life, she'd changed his too.

Chapter Three

Laughing would probably be a bad idea, but the look on his brother's face made Jackson want to laugh anyway. His brother's expression reminded him of the time he'd covered a bagel with frosting and sprinkles to make it look like a donut. He really didn't think anyone would fall for it. James had and he hadn't found it funny.

And Jackson knew what was happening now wasn't funny either, but he still had to bite his lip.

James stood in the middle of the bedroom with his hands on his hips and glared at him. "Why didn't you tell me you had a wife?"

Jackson opened his dresser drawer. Putting on some more clothes was probably a good idea. "I didn't know I had a wife. I mean I forgot I had a wife. I don't know what's going on. I woke up with…" Jackson closed his eyes and pounded his forehead with his fist. "I should know her name."

"Yes, you should," James said in a dry tone. "It's Enomwoyi."

Jackson stared at him. "En-no what?"

"En-nohm-WHO-yee."

Jackson swore. He'd never have guessed that. "How did you remember that?"

"She introduced herself to me at the party last night, but that's not the point. Who is *she*?"

Jackson tapped his chest. "You just told me. She's someone I met last night." The charity party had been more interesting than he'd expected it to be. He couldn't stop a grin as he walked into his closet. His brother liked to tease him that it was the size of an Olympic swimming pool. "She was amazing. She could do this thing with her lips that—"

"Not Enomwoyi," James said with a frown as he followed him, "your wife."

Jackson folded his arms and let his gaze skim over his selection of shirts then sweaters. "Oh, right. Her."

"Yes, her! Mrs. Jackson Fortune. Do you realize what you've done?"

"Right," he said absently. Should today be an orange or yellow day? He turned sharply when he heard his brother swear before he grabbed three shirts and put them in another location. "What are you doing?" Jackson demanded. He took the shirts and put them back in place. When it came to his clothes he had a precise order. They were arranged by size, color, season and material.

"Getting you to pay attention."

"You're the one who told me not to go around in my robe."

James reached for another shirt.

Jackson held up his hands in surrender. "I'm listening. I'm listening."

"What happened?"

"I'm not sure yet."

"That's not good enough. You need a good story to tell Edgar."

Jackson sighed at the mention of their stepfather. Their stepfather, Edgar Fortune, was founder of BioMed Solutions, a company that manufactured joint replacements. While not a sexy business, with a growing aging population with more active lives, business was booming.

Edgar had eclipsed any memory they'd had of their Grenadian father who'd left their lives a year after their younger brother Rudy was born with Down syndrome.

Edgar had adopted them and they'd lost their last name "Brownson" and had become Fortunes. Edgar liked to constantly remind them, "I gave you my name for a reason. It means your fortunes have changed. So you owe everything to me." He had drilled into them the importance of maintaining a good reputation. Jackson hadn't always been as diligent as his brother, but he'd never gotten into trouble like this before. Neither of them liked displeasing him.

At six-years-old Jackson had been in awe of the Jamaican born-US raised man who loved Cuban cigars, boxing and fast horses. His awe soon turned to affection, although it had taken years to warm up to him. Edgar was a driven, ruthless man and a hard man to get close to and had surprised many by marrying a woman with three kids. After their mother's passing last year, he'd softened a little, but not enough to look past a mistake like this.

Angering Edgar was never a good idea. "I will give him the perfect story."

"At least tell me you got a prenup," James said.

Jackson rubbed his forehead.

James read his expression and swore. He stormed farther into the large closet, grabbed a bunch of shirts and threw them on the ground.

Jackson raced after him and gathered them up like they were precious gems. "Not the clothes. Not the clothes! Take it out on me."

James grabbed him by the lapels of his robe and shook him. "You want Edgar to kill you?"

"Relax," Jackson said with a nervous laugh, "this is what lawyers are for. Trust me. I can handle this. I'll pay her off and get rid of her quietly. No one needs to know."

James patted him on the cheek and flashed a sour grin. "You haven't woken up yet, have you?"

"What do you mean?"

He rested his hands on his hips. "Why do you think I'm here?"

"I don't know."

James pulled out his cell phone then showed Jackson an online posting with the heading *Fortune Finds a Bride!* and a picture of Jackson and Toyin smiling in front of a chapel.

Jackson stared at the image appalled. "How did this happen?"

"You tell me."

"Why did I wear that shirt? It looks awful against—"

James snatched the cell phone from him. He walked to a silk cream colored shirt Jackson hadn't picked up off the ground and stomped on it, leaving a footprint. "That's not the point." He stomped on it again.

Jackson shook with anger as he stared at the damage. He kept his voice low. "What is wrong with you?"

James's brows shot up. "What's wrong with me? My brother is an idiot!"

Jackson gathered the rest of the shirts and placed them on the bed, separating what would have to be dry cleaned and ironed. "We could just squash it as a rumor. Get the lawyers on it."

"It won't be that easy."

"In the meantime I just need you to do me a favor. Someone needs to deal with her." He pointed to James's jacket. "Let me—"

James laughed. "Don't even think about it," he said, reading his brother's mind. "I'm never switching places with you again. I took care of one wife for you, this time you're on your own."

"I thought you came here to help me."

"No, I came here to warn you."

"About what?"

"Edgar collapsed last night after the event. He's okay now," James quickly said, seeing the concern on his brother's face, "but you know Mom's passing hit him hard. He can't take any more stress."

"So you're saying he doesn't know?"

"Not yet. We need a quick, simple solution."

Jackson grinned. "You leave that to me." When his brother looked unconvinced he frowned. "What?"

"You haven't been yourself since…"

"Since what?"

"You know what."

"I'm fine." Jackson held up the ruined shirt. "Except when my brother goes crazy and does this."

James's blinked, unmoved. "You have six others."

"They're not the same."

"White is white."

Jackson waved his hand. "Don't go there with me." He and his brother never agreed when it came to clothes, food, art or entertainment. "Mom's passing was a surprise for all of us, but I'm moving on. I haven't changed."

James's tone softened. "Three assistants in six months?"

"Bo's stayed so far," Jackson said, seeking some credit. He knew he'd given his past assistants a hard time—changing his schedule without warning, at times losing his temper. "I've improved."

"You call a wedding in Vegas an improvement? What is going on with you?"

Jackson shrugged. "Living life to the fullest."

"Recklessly."

Jackson went into the closet again and grabbed a pair of dark purple trousers. "I don't need a lecture."

"I'm not only here because of Edgar. It's Ava. She's been talking to Edgar about…about possibly removing you as head of marketing."

Jackson sat down hard on the bed as if he'd been punched in the gut.

"It wouldn't be permanent," James continued, "just for a couple of months until you…get yourself together."

Jackson glared at him. "Talk about holding a grudge! That woman has had it in it for me since—"

"I agree with her."

For a moment Jackson lost the power to speak. Words filled his mind but the pain of his brother's betrayal stopped them from leaving his mouth. He swallowed then said in a hoarse voice, "You what?"

James sighed with regret. "I agree with her."

Jackson surged to his feet. "You want to see me kicked out of our company? A company you and I have helped build? You're throwing me over for her?"

"It's not throwing you over. If it were just your personal life then I would defend you, but you've made critical public mistakes that have affected the company. When your choices affect other's livelihood I can't sit back. It's not good for all of us."

Jackson pulled on his trousers. "Mistakes happen."

"Want to say that to Edgar?"

He knew what his stepfather would say. He didn't mind mistakes as long as they weren't lazy ones and Jackson's had been the worst kind. In a rush he'd sent out a typo filled memo and another with an image inserted upside down; at the last minute he'd stopped himself before sending out a huge email marketing push to the wrong subscriber list.

But the worst had been the recent disastrous new logo launch which he'd pushed for to expand the brand, an unnecessary and costly decision. The new logo had lasted an amazing two days before its demise at the hands of a public outcry. They hated the look and what they thought it represented. It was only in hindsight that he realized he'd gotten out of touch with their core base and had ignored the feeling towards the brand. He'd been too focused on the numbers: Blinded by software that focused on customer relationship management instead of what was truly important—the actual *people* behind the data. He wasn't used to feeling embarrassed, but he was and knew his brother had a right to be worried. Which only angered him more.

He selected a purple and white geometric shirt and put it on. "I'm good at what I do."

"You used to be."

James's words hurt, but Jackson knew his brother was right. He hadn't been as topnotch as he'd been before his brother's marriage to Ava and his mother's passing. Both had hit him hard—Ava's initial hidden agenda against the Fortune family and their mother succumbing to cancer faster than they'd expected. He didn't want to admit how unmoored he'd felt since last year. It embarrassed him that others had noticed too. He was thirty-five; he should have his life under control.

"I'm not going to let her force me out."

"She's thinking about the company."

"I don't believe that. She's thinking about her investment. Her reputation." Ava's arrival in their lives, both personally and professionally, had come at an opportune time. The agent Ava's company had developed was a biodegradable solution that allowed replaced joints to stay in place longer and to eventually be replaced by the patient's own cells within two or three years. It had given BioMed Solutions the extra value to please stockholders. And her marriage to James had also given the company's image a boost. Both events had pleased Edgar immensely.

"Maybe it's time to start thinking about yours."

Jackson held up his hand. "Enough. You win."

"This isn't a game."

"Then why do I feel as if I've already lost?"

"Jackson, listen—"

"No, you can't let her—" He took a deep breath, not wanting to show his anger. "You have to take my side in this." He held his brother's gaze, pleading. "This is all I have. What am I supposed to do? Huh? Mom used to tell me how proud she was of me, of us…I won't let Ava take this way from me."

"Then stop giving her ammunition. I told her not to tell Edgar about this marriage fiasco and I've made sure he won't hear about it for at least a few days, but time isn't on your side." James held up his hand before Jackson could speak. "I will give you a second chance and let you stay as head of marketing, if you do one thing. Show me you're the same guy who did Operation Domination."

Jackson couldn't stop a smile. He hadn't heard that phrase for so long for a moment he didn't know what his brother was talking about. Then it all came back to him. The person he used to be. Someone he'd forgotten.

Seventeen years ago, as a freshman in college, he'd wanted to prove to Edgar that he had the skill to be hired by the company in the marketing division. So he'd given himself a challenge and told Edgar about it. He'd pledge the worse fraternity on campus and then turn it into the best. He'd achieve his mission by using valid marketing strategies to increase its membership by hosting four get acquainted parties. He wanted to convince students to join *his* fraternity above all others.

So using his basic understanding of why guys joined fraternities—mainly to meet girls and a sense of brotherhood—he set out to prove that his fraternity had it all. When his first attempts to invite the most sexy and beautiful girls on campus to act as hostesses at parties failed, he decided to hire five of the most beautiful strippers from two local strip clubs. They were eager to pretend to be sexy coeds and hostesses for his parties. He also had the guys practice pretending to be "brotherly" when in most cases they couldn't stand each other. By the time he launched the fraternity's first party they looked like the most connected group of guys with the hottest women around.

He ended up with the biggest pledge class in the school's history, by the time the fourth party occurred they didn't have enough room for everyone and the strippers had such a good time that they invited their girlfriends to come and party too. He'd impressed everyone, especially Edgar. He'd succeeded at both goals.

Could he do something like that again? He knew it wasn't a real question. He didn't have a choice. He flashed his brother a smile and tugged on the cuffs of his shirt, ready to lie. "You can trust me. I've got it all under control."

Chapter Four

"You know I want to trust you," James said, following Jackson down the hall towards the living room, "but then you do crazy things like get married and sleep with women whose name you don't remember the next morning, I get worried."

Jackson shook his head impressed. "I don't know how you were able to remember her name, but it wasn't going to be a one night stand. I liked Eno…uh you know. Not only is she beautiful, but she is smart and that accent—"

"The accent is fake," Toyin said.

The brothers stopped in the entryway and stared at her. Toyin looked at their startled faces and waved her hand. "Sorry, none of my business."

"What do you mean the accent is fake?" James said, taking a step forward.

"It's very good, but before she left, someone called her and I overheard her on the phone and her accent was gone."

James hung his head. "Damn. The curse strikes again."

"Curse?" Toyin said.

"It's nothing," Jackson said with a grin.

"Nothing?" James said. "In a vat of a thousand, you'd find the one rotten apple."

"She probably was just trying to impress us."

"Then why did she try to take your USB?" Toyin asked.

"USB?" the brothers said in unison.

Toyin nodded. "Yes, it was on the table and I thought it was strange when she came and briefly talked to me before she left."

James sat down in front of her, intrigued. "She spoke to you?"

"Yes, she was saying how sorry she was. That she didn't know Jackson was married. At first I thought she was truly distressed until I noticed that when she passed by that coffee table—"

"It's a cocktail table," Jackson said.

"They're the same thing," James said.

"No, coffee tables are thicker and sturdier. Look at these fine lines."

James turned to Toyin and pointed to Jackson. "As you can see my brother gets easily distracted by nonessentials."

"It's not—"

"What happened?" James interrupted.

"The USB was gone," Toyin said.

James swore. Jackson sunk into the couch and stared at the table.

"Who does she work for?" James asked him.

"I don't know. I think it was some medical firm. She said she was worried she might get fired if their sales didn't increase soon."

"And that didn't raise alarm bells?"

Jackson looked up at him. "Why would it?"

"What was on the USB?" James asked.

Jackson shook his head.

"Tell me what was on it."

He stood and paced. "A special campaign project the team was working on. I—"

"Don't worry," Toyin said, holding up the item. "She didn't leave with it." She stood up and set the item down on the table.

The same moment James seized the USB, Jackson walked over to Toyin and whispered, "Just play along and pretend that you love me," before he turned to his brother and said, "She's lying."

James looked up at him, startled. "What?"

Jackson turned to her, his eyes dark. "Aren't you?"

Toyin blinked not knowing what to say. Shocked by his sudden change. At first she'd feared his brother now she wasn't sure of him. "I…"

"You're upset because you found me with another woman and you want to discredit her," Jackson said. "Isn't that it?"

She swallowed and licked her lips. "No," she said, drawing out the word, trying to think of what to say in response.

"I wasn't lying. I knew she was bad for you the moment I saw her and…don't you remember? That's why you married me."

The two men looked at her openmouthed.

She took that moment to expand on her lie. "You wanted me to keep you safe from gold diggers and users because you thought you were cursed," she added, remembering what his brother had just said. "Of course I didn't think I'd fall in love with you on top of it."

"Wait, sit down," James said. "Are you telling me my brother planned this?"

She nodded, but didn't sit, feeling uncomfortable with Jackson standing so close to her and staring at her as if she'd grown a second head. "He was drunk at the time, yes, so I'm not surprised he doesn't remember, but he asked me to be his secret weapon. He told me how he's had bad luck with women and that he needed a weapon to keep him out of trouble. 'If only I had a wife,' " she said, deepening his voice to mimic his. She shot him a glance. "Yes, that's what you said and I said 'Could it be anyone?' and you said 'Sure'. I was also a little tipsy and recovering from a breakup so we did the deed. No one was supposed to know, but it leaked when my sister saw the pictures on my cell phone. We've been secretly seeing each other for two months."

"I don't believe this," James said. "How long were you going to keep this up?"

"I don't know," Toyin said, wondering how to strengthen her lie. "Jackson thought he needed several months to get over his bad luck. I didn't realize he'd already fallen off track or I would have been here sooner. That's part of why I announced our marriage so that I could keep him safe from other women."

James frowned. "I thought you said your sister leaked it?"

Oops, yes, she'd forgotten about that. Best to stick to one story. "She did, but only because I was thinking about it."

"You didn't come here for an annulment?"

"I don't want his money," Toyin said quickly, wishing Jackson would say something so she could stop digging herself in deeper. "Don't worry about that. I truly do…uh…c-care about him, although I know he doesn't feel the same about me. I just wanted to help."

James clapped his hands together, jumped up and laughed. "You got me!" He hugged his brother. "I should have known this was one of your tricks and if I hadn't been so relieved I would be furious. You really made me believe—" He shook his head, grinned and slapped his brother on the back. "You sly dog. You had me really worried for a minute. She's perfect. Why didn't you just tell me the truth?"

Jackson plastered on a smile. "You know I don't think sharp in the morning."

"It's nearly noon." James turned to Toyin. "You're right. My brother has a soft spot that makes him vulnerable. You're exactly what he needs right now."

Toyin took Jackson's hand and gazed up at him with a look of longing. "If only he felt the same."

Humor touched his eyes and he bit his lip.

She narrowed her gaze daring him to laugh.

Jackson squeezed her hand and looked away, but she saw his shoulders shake.

"This is amazing," James said. "We need you to expand on this."

Jackson looked at him uncertain, all humor gone. "Expand on what?"

"This charade. No more secret meetings. She has to move in with you and you have to make it real." James rested his hands on his hips. "I'm proud of you. A true winner. I don't know how you managed it, but you found a woman who's sincere. She hasn't asked for money, she won't mention anything about Enomwoyi and when the timing is right she's willing to annul this quietly. I think that says a lot about her. She's great for your image. She'll give you a look of stability. She can keep the gold diggers away. Plus, with Edgar in a bad way right now, he could use good news."

"I'll only do it on one condition."

"What?"

"No suspension. Not even briefly."

"I'll talk to Ava."

"No, I'm talking to you." He held out his hand. "Do we have a deal?"

James sighed then nodded and shook his hand. "We do."

Jackson smiled. "Good."

"I'll get going now."

"Bye. Tell Ava where she can put her broom."

James laughed used to his brother's good natured teasing. "Talk to you soon," he said then left.

"What just happened?" Toyin asked after James had gone.

Jackson turned to Toyin. "You just saved my life," he said then pulled her close and covered her mouth with his.

Chapter Five

The surprise alone should have stopped her from responding but her body did anyway. It savored the soft, warm feel of his lips against hers. One arm encircling her waist, bringing her body close to his. One hand soft as it slid down the back of her neck, in direct contrast to his body which was hard. Solid. Hot. The heat penetrating his shirt and hers, making her temperature rise. The sweet, savage assault of his mouth, causing shivers of delight to race through her.

Jackson drew away, licked his lips, as if savoring the final taste of a good meal and let his hand slid down her hip, "Yes," he said in a low hiss. "I remember this." He kissed her again, quick and a little wild before he said in wonder, "I'm in love."

"Wh-what?" she stammered, breathless.

His dark eyes searched her face. "I know you, but you look different."

"Jackson," she said unable to say anything more than his name.

"Why isn't it coming together? I've never felt like this with anyone."

"What just happened?"

"I don't know," he said with feeling. "Let's try it again." He bent to kiss her.

Toyin pressed her hand against his chest, stopping him. "Not the kiss. Your brother."

He drew her close. "Let's discuss him later."

She struggled to free herself, annoyed that she liked the feel of his hands around her. "Stop it. You were just with another woman."

"I know. I'm sorry. I forgot it was like this."

She wiggled out of his grasp and took a hasty step back, desperate for distance. "Jackson, be serious."

"I am. You felt it too, right?"

"No," she lied, wishing her lips didn't tingle. That her body didn't remember every place where his hands had been. "Now sit down and tell me what's going on. Why did you want me to pretend I loved you?"

Jackson looked at her for a long moment then nodded resigned, but he didn't sit down. Instead he folded his arms. "Nobody can ever know about Eno…whatsit."

"Enomwoyi."

His brows shot up. "You remember her name too?"

It was easy to remember the name of the gorgeous Amazon who made her feel as appealing as a tree stump. "Yes, go on."

He rubbed the back of his neck. "I have a habit of finding women who want to use me. In the past it wasn't a big deal, but now I can't afford it." He frowned. "You don't look surprise."

"Why would I be? You told me this two months ago."

He looked sheepish. "I talked a lot, didn't I?"

She nodded.

"So I must have told you about Ava."

"The woman you were supposed to marry, but who ended up marrying your brother instead?"

"Yes, that's her. Recently, I've made some mistakes and that would give her just what she needs to get rid of me."

Toyin paused, surprised. "You think she's trying to get your brother to push you out of the business?"

"No, unfortunately, I don't think it's that simple. The truth is my family thinks I'm a liability and I need to prove that I'm not. I will pay you enough to make this worth your while to play this charade for a couple more months." He motioned her towards him.

She took a hesitant step forward. "What is it?"

"I want to kiss you again and see if I remember anything else."

She was tempted, but knew he was too charming to toy with. Even his casual remark of being "in love" already had her heart racing and her mind running wild. There was no way he was being serious and she couldn't let herself fall for him. "No, it won't help. You wouldn't remember anything by kissing me anyway."

"Why not?"

"Because we didn't kiss in Vegas."

"Really?" He laughed. "I married you and I didn't kiss you? That doesn't sound like me."

He was right. She was lying, but if he could barely even remember who she was she wasn't going to remind him of a kiss that still had her mouth burning even more so than the brief one he'd just given her now. It was clear she was one of many.

"You look both familiar and strange at the same time." He stopped and stared at a napkin she'd left on the table. When Reginald had given her a drink he'd offered her the napkin which, out of boredom, she'd used to sketch a squirrel with numb chucks. Jackson lifted it up then looked at her. "Take off the wig."

Her hand shot to her head; her face burned. "What? How do you know I'm wearing a wig?"

"Because it's not a very good one." He sat down and winked up at her. "You can relax, Toyin. I remember you. I was teasing."

She sat down in front of him and folded her arms. She was not taking off the wig. "Were you pretending the entire time?"

"No, not the entire time. Take off the lashes too." He motioned to her clothes. "Why did you dress up like that anyway?"

It had been her sister's idea. Toyin usually wore jeans and a shirt, kept her shoulder length black hair in twists, wore black, square glasses and barely any makeup. At times, for fun, she would put on a pink or silver wig and lipstick to match. But her sister didn't think that was posh enough, so she shoved Toyin in a fitted skirt and blouse, wig, contacts and false lashes and enough makeup to make her face feel like it was falling under the weight of it. "I thought if I was going to pretend to be your wife I have to play the part."

"Technically you are my wife. So you don't have to pretend."

"I wanted to make an impression."

"It's the wrong one; you look a little too…" He waved his hand searching for words. "Much. And that's saying a lot coming from me. But we'll work on that later."

"Your brother liked me, remember?"

"My brother thinks there's only one type of white," Jackson said in disgust.

"Technically, he's right," she said, stretching the word "technically" the way he had. "But there are shades of white like vanilla, cream and eggshell. Just as there are shades of brown like chestnut and beaver or orange such as peach and apricot…what?" she said when he stared at her strangely. "Sorry, I know I can go on."

"No, it's nice. You understand me. Most people don't understand the language of color. How important it is."

"I took a course on color theory."

He grinned, his eyes warm. "Me too." His grin fell. "Which is why you should know that wig is too black for

your skin tone and drowns out the soft red undertone of
your skin."

The way his gaze made a slow descent down her body,
made her skin tingle. She didn't know how he managed to
make a criticism feel sensual but he did. Her face burned.
"I'll take it off later." Toyin adjusted the wig, resisting the
urge to scratch, her head felt hot.

"You can at least take off the lashes."

"You'd probably want me to take my clothes off too."

He leaned forward and let his voice drop. "Only if you
insist."

She couldn't help a laugh. "No."

His eyes held hers, his dark gaze taking her in. "You're
fine just the way you are."

Toyin turned away unable to hold his gaze. He was dangerous. How could he so easily flirt with her after waking up
with another woman?

Jackson clasped his hands together and rested his chin
on top of them. "It was just sex."

She looked at him again. "What?"

"I like having sex. That's all it was." He shook his head.
"No, I'm not a mind reader, I'm just good at reading faces."

"Then why are you so bad at choosing women?"

He let his hands fall and shrugged. "Don't know."

"So you do remember what happened?"

He grinned. "Enough."

She wasn't sure she liked the gleam in his eyes. That was how she'd ended up married to him in the first place. He was a true mischief maker and she wasn't sure she wanted to be part of the chaos he could create. The offer of money sounded good, but would it be enough to deal with any long term consequences?

"I'll take care of you," he said.

"What?"

"You looked worried and I'm telling you not to be." He offered her a generous financial amount.

Toyin stared at him amazed.

"Will that make everything worth it? I need you. I told you, I have to prove myself. I am also worried about my stepfather's health and…you won't have to do much. I'm sure you could use the money."

"Why would you say that?"

He shrugged. "Most people do."

Her sister was right. She needed the money and this was her chance. She could use the money to hire the lawyers she needed and recoup what was left of TJ Studios and possibly start again. And the landlord had threatened to raise the rent on her store because of its excellent location. He'd ignored her pleas to let her buy the property out right.

She was desperate, but there was also something suspicious about all this. About the casual way he mentioned her needing funds. She didn't remember telling him about her money problems, but perhaps he'd made a lucky guess. She wouldn't overthink it. She could just hear her sister scolding her for giving up a good opportunity. What would be so hard about being married to a wealthy guy for a few months?

"Okay," she said, "I'll do it on one condition."

"Go ahead."

"Never say you love me. Not in jest and definitely not for real."

He laughed. "You're joking, right?"

She didn't smile. "No, that's my condition."

Jackson stared at her for a long moment then shook his head. "Sorry, come up with something else."

Toyin blinked, stunned by his response. "Why?"

"Because I'm going to slip and say 'I love you.' I can't help myself."

"Try."

"No."

"But you don't."

He shrugged.

"I don't like when people cheapen such a powerful word by using it all the time."

He shrugged again, unfazed. "I can't help that I love a lot of things."

"Like women and wine?"

He placed a hand over his heart. "Ouch."

"I take words seriously." When his expression didn't change she sighed. He'd be harder to defeat than her sister.

"Fine, you can say whatever you want, but don't expect me to say that I love you."

"No, that's part of the deal."

"I'll act like I love you, but I won't say it."

"I'll pay you fifty dollars each time you say it. A maximum of three hundred a day. Not to be said consecutively. They must be spaced."

"You're not serious."

"I'm offering money, of course I'm serious."

"Who says 'I love you' to someone six times a day?"

"You," he said with a wink, "if it's worth your while."

Toyin briefly hung her head. "I'm not winning this argument, am I?"

"This is a negotiation not an argument."

She lifted her head. "Okay, deal."

"Good, any other conditions?"

"I'm not sleeping with you."

He merely smiled, but his smile said 'yet' and she didn't want to argue. He'd already outmaneuvered her twice.

She'd have to make sure to never sleep with him and under no circumstances to fall for him. Ever. He was certainly handsome and could be charming, but he could also be cunning and reckless. No woman in her right mind would give her heart to a man like him. She could save her business and after the charade was over she'd never have to see him again.

"If you're with other women be discreet," she said.

"There won't be other women."

He sounded sincere, but she didn't dare believe him. "I don't care what you do. Just don't humiliate me until this charade is over."

She expected him to argue. Instead he took her hand and kissed the back of it. "Your wish is my command," he said then a slow smile spread across his lips.

And her traitorous heart responded. It was that same mischievous expression that had gotten her into this mess two months ago…

Chapter Six

Las Vegas, two months ago

She wouldn't cry. Toyin took a long swallow of her whiskey, then set the glass on the laminated plastic bar, ignoring the happy chatter around her. No matter how much it hurt she wouldn't shed a tear. She'd be stoic, resolute.

She would not cry about her boyfriend running off with her business manager and leaving her alone in a Las Vegas hotel where they'd planned to elope.

She wouldn't cry because she'd believed the words he'd told her only a few hours ago.

"I love you more than you know," he'd said after they'd left the comic conference room together that morning. They'd come to the multi-day event in Las Vegas for both business development and a chance to network with other trade and creative professionals in the industry, meeting long-standing and upcoming artists, colorists, inkers, editors, producers and publishers. She'd felt charged by the atmosphere and couldn't wait to go home and use the knowledge and new connections she'd been able to make.

"I know," Toyin said, thinking that the creative buzz had influenced him. "Hasn't it been a great conference?"

She watched people dressed up as Captain America, Deadpool and Elsa the Snow Queen walk pass them.

He tugged on her sleeve to get her attention. "We're here. So let's do it."

She looked at him confused. "Let's do what?"

"Get married. Let's do something impulsive. I don't see myself spending my life with anyone else."

And in her madness she'd agreed. They'd been dating for nearly two years. It seemed the right move. He loved her. Wasn't that enough? Plus, pressure from her family had become unbearable. Her Nigerian grandmother had sent her three photos of possible matches. Every time Toyin deleted them from her phone, more kept coming, like a bad infection.

"I'm already in a relationship," she'd told her grandmother before her trip to Vegas. Her grandmother had stopped by her store to scold her for skipping out on her cousin's baby shower. She'd skipped it on purpose because she knew that her grandmother had someone she'd wanted to introduce to her.

Mama Bisi, as her grandmother was affectionately called, was a powerful matriarch. A woman whose beauty was more of an illusion than an actuality. She had a cool grace and stark features and was the mother of three sons (all doctors) and two daughters (both engineers), Toyin's mother being one. She had the height and breadth of a monarch and the gift of a seer. She'd been able to match all her children (Toyin's mother having been advantageously matched with a black British Cambridge student) and now had set her sights on her grandchildren and no one interfered with her rulings.

Mama Bisi had been instrumental in helping her sister, Maryam get married, and her brother, Kemi, was prepared to be matched with whomever she chose. But Toyin had flouted tradition when she'd fallen for Lance, although her grandmother didn't like him. He was of average height and far from handsome, but earnest and smart. He had a slightly nasal voice that she found endearing. But he supported her and believed in her vision for the future.

"You're not in a relationship," her grandmother scoffed with a dismissive wave of her hand. "You're in a holding pen. Will he marry you or not?"

Toyin looked around the store, keeping her voice low. Hoping no one could overhear them. "Right now I'm still focused on my TJ Studios." She walked towards the back office.

"Why did you have to add to your troubles? A family will keep you busy enough. Your little store and cartoons were plenty and then you get yourself into debt with this other nonsense."

Toyin walked into the office and lifted a box from a chair until she noticed the stuffing coming out from a hole in the seat. She set the box back down and moved books from another. "It's not nonsense. It's something I love."

Her grandmother took a seat, looking around the cramped office in distaste. "You need to find a man to love too."

"I'm with Lance."

"But you don't love him."

Toyin sighed. "I do in my own way."

"I know why you put all your heart in creating a business here a project there and nothing else. It's because you're bored. A woman your age would be. You need another creative outlet and that's what a family is for."

Toyin bit the inside of her cheek not wanting to be rude. Her grandmother had never understood her or her ambitions. She'd been openly heartbroken that she hadn't gone into engineering; although it was clear to everyone she'd never had the interest. "I wanted to do this because it's been a dream of mine."

"Do you want children?"

"Someday."

"Someday doesn't exist on the calendar. You need to grow up."

"I am grown." She hated how her grandmother treated her as if she weren't fully grown without a man and baby on her hip.

"You have to make him marry you or find someone else."

Her grandmother's words echoed in her mind when Lance offered her his sudden proposal. It had come at the best time. She could now show her family that she could be both a wife, a passionate artist and businesswoman. This wedding would prove her grandmother wrong. That she hadn't wasted her time with Lance and that she was an adult and had "settled down" as they so often liked to tell her.

Perhaps the otherworldly feel of the conference—the colorful costumes, the feel of possibility—had also influenced her decision, but against her better judgment she'd agreed to marry him.

The fact that he'd disappeared for the next several hours should have been her first clue that something was wrong. That perhaps he wasn't as committed to a new life together as he'd seemed. But he'd disappeared on her before. Once when she'd sprained her wrist and had to give up a major commission and another time when she'd gotten the client from hell. Both times, instead of being there for her, he'd sent her flowers and his apologies for being so busy (he was working on his PhD) so she hadn't paid much attention.

After he proposed, he'd told her he had some business to take care of first (he worked for a small publishing company) and that he couldn't wait to see her as his bride later that day when they scheduled to meet. She'd believed him. She'd booked the chapel, extended their hotel stay and planned everything. She even contacted one of the costume retailers at the conference to help her and managed to create a Corpse Bride costume. All he had to do was show up.

Which he did.

With someone else.

Toyin wasn't supposed to catch him in the lobby with the pretty woman by his side. Her business manager, Shanna. Lance had planned to meet her in their hotel room, but Toyin had been eager to meet him. So she'd left a half hour early and decided to wait for him in the lobby.

Which meant she wasn't supposed to overhear him talking to Shanna about his plans.

"Relax," he told her in a sexy voice he'd never used with Toyin. "There's nothing to worry about. If she sees you, just say you attended the conference too."

"You're really going to marry her?"

"It makes sense, but it won't interfere with us. You know I'd never give you up. She doesn't know anything about us and this is the best way to handle it. Once she finds out what you plan she'll be on the warpath. But as her husband I can control her and I'll have access to key information and intellectual property. You wouldn't believe the assets she has that she doesn't know how to manage. We can both live off of her."

"I just don't think it's good that I stay in the same hotel."

"She'll be happy to see you and you'll be our witness. Baby, I've got this all under control."

Toyin stumbled away from the lobby. She wouldn't find out the full extent of the damage Shanna had done until she returned home. For now, all her mind could focus on was Lance's betrayal. She hurried back to her hotel room and lost her lunch, but she didn't cry, her mind spinning on what to do.

She thought of poisoning the champagne and chocolates she had bought to celebrate; stuffing the roses she'd gotten in his mouth and stabbing him with an ice pick. She'd charged everything on a credit card, because Lance had told her he was buried under too many student loans to get into any more debt, and now she had nothing to show for it.

She didn't confront him when he arrived back in their hotel room, wearing her favorite cologne. She kissed him and pretended that everything was fine. She even considered sleeping with him so that at the height of climax she could twist her body in a way that would break his penis. But she decided that would be too dramatic. She didn't want to deal with an emergency room visit. Instead, she said, "How long have you been dipping your pen in Shanna's ink well?"

"What?"

"How long have you been with Shanna?"

He shook his head and sat down on the bed. "I don't know what you're talking about."

"I overheard you in the lobby. Shanna was right, you shouldn't have brought her here. Otherwise I would have never known."

"She's blackmailing me."

"Don't make me laugh."

"It's true, there are something's in my past—"

Toyin gripped her hands together and lowered her head as if in pain. "I don't want to go to prison." She glared at him. "But if you keep talking, I'm afraid I'm going to kill you."

Something in her gaze made him believe her. He slowly stood. "Whatever you're thinking, it wasn't like that."

"I will make you pay."

"Toyin."

"Not tonight, not this year, but you'd better hide because when I get over this…you will wish you were dead."

Lance smiled, his nasal voice taking on an ugly tone. "The trouble with you is that you live in comics. Revenge? Really? By the time you recover from this, we'll both be in rocking chairs. You need me if you want to survive what's in store."

"I don't need you," Toyin said, not realizing the truth of his words. "Now or ever."

Minutes later Toyin found herself at the hotel bar wondering what she would do next. She didn't want to think about his veiled threat or what he and Shanna had been up to.

She dreaded returning home to face it. At thirty-two she was already the family loser and this breakup would prove them right. She pulled out her cell phone and with her finger, sketched herself as a horse inside a stable. Her grandmother had been right, Lance had been riding her until he found someone else to replace her and she'd been left with nothing. The cheating hurt, but why did he have to make fun of her dream? She lived in comics?

He knew that wasn't true. Just because drawing comics was a passion didn't mean she was delusional. She'd thought he'd been different. He was one of the few people she'd trusted with her comic ideas and web animations. Why had he said he loved her? Why did he have to use that cruel lie? She had loved him in her own way. She'd felt safe with him. But he'd used her. Tears stung her eyes.

Toyin blinked them away. No she wouldn't cry. Love was for losers. Falling for him had been stupid. She'd never be stupid again.

Toyin felt a tap on her shoulder and looked up into the dark, magnetic brown eyes of a handsome man who seemed to make the rest of the world fall away. He reminded her of someone but she wasn't sure who.

"What's wrong, Beautiful?" he said.

Chapter Seven

His words made the world come back into cruel focus, the sound of laughter from a trio in the corner and the clink of glasses against the table assaulting her ears. Great, now someone was making fun of her.

She flashed a sour grin. "Are you trying to be funny?"

He blinked. "No."

"Good, because you failed. Now leave me alone."

"I didn't mean…I'm sorry," he said. "I just wanted to know why."

She rolled her eyes. "Why what?"

"What's a bride doing sitting at a bar all alone?"

"How do you know I'm a bride?"

He tapped the side of his head. "Because I'm psychic."

"Really?"

He motioned to her clothes. "And the wedding dress was a clue."

Toyin looked down at her dress horrified. She'd forgotten to change. She'd left the hotel room wanting to get as far away from Lance as she could. She'd gone around looking like a bride raised from the dead. She must look pathetic. "It's a long story." She looked over his three piece sharkskin metallic blue suit with a flashy red shirt. She couldn't guess what character he was trying to imitate. "Did you attend the conference too?"

"What?"

She shook her head. "Never mind."

"I'm interested in that long story you have to tell. I'll get us a table and you can tell me about it."

She laughed. No way was she going to fall for that act. "I don't have money, I'm not interested in sex and my family isn't rich."

The man frowned. "What does that have to do with anything?"

"I don't know what game you're playing but I'm not interested."

"Game?"

"A gorgeous man picks up a lonely woman at a bar. Wine and dines her. Listens to her sob stories, makes her feel as if he's 'The One' then starts a rebound romance that costs her money and her self-respect."

He leaned on the bar, resting his cheek against his fist. "Wow, I've never heard that before."

"I have."

He straightened. "Well, you did get one thing right. I am gorgeous, but I don't want anything from you. I have my own money, I work for my family business and I've given up women…for a while."

She paused. She hadn't expected that. She looked him up and down again. A man like him, giving up on women? "Why?"

He grinned. "You first."

He had her there. She was curious. Very curious. The storyteller in her found the promise of what he had to say irresistible. It could have been a ploy, but his disarming grin persuaded her that he had a story to tell and she didn't want to sit alone or go back to her room.

He held out his hand. "My name is Jackson Fortune, by the way."

"I've never heard that character before. What's his back story?"

He paused. "Back story?"

"Isn't Jackson Fortune who you're pretending to be?"

"Pretending?"

"Your costume and your name."

He glanced down at his clothes then looked up at her confused. "I'm not wearing a costume. And I just told you my real name."

She felt her face burn. "Oh sorry. I didn't mean…You really…uh look amazing."

"Thank you." He held his hand out again. "And your name is?"

She shook his hand, momentarily entranced by his steady gaze. "Toyin Jackson…I mean Fortune." She shook her head. "Jacobs. Toyin Jacobs."

"Actually, Toyin Fortune has a nice ring to it."

She narrowed her gaze, trying to resist his flirtation. "I thought you were giving up women."

"I am…slowly."

She jumped down from the bar stool. "And I'm starving."

"Order what you want. I'm paying."

After having Lance deceive her she wasn't sure he wouldn't excuse himself to the restroom and never return. But then he said as if reading her mind, "You can look me up if you want."

"No, that's okay. I'm ready to take a gamble."

Moments later they sat in a restaurant booth with two orders of shrimp scampi, the bread basket filled with hot rolls, and Toyin briefly telling Jackson about her ruined wedding plans. She reached for the salt.

Jackson stopped her. "Don't insult the chef. Try the food first."

"I like salt."

"Probably because you've lost the ability to taste. I bet you soak your sushi in soy sauce."

"I don't eat sushi."

"And the world thanks you. It's best not to eat it than to destroy it."

She studied him for a moment. "Are you a chef by any chance?"

"No, just a man who enjoys food." He nodded to her plate. "Just try it."

She took a bite then set her fork down. "You're right. My taste buds are dead. Can I have the salt now?"

Jackson took a taste of his food then visibly shuddered. "Too much oil, not enough garlic and the parsley hasn't been fresh in years. You're right. There's no flavor."

Toyin lifted the salt shaker. "There will be in a minute."

He motioned to the waiter. "No, wait. We're not eating here."

"We're not?"

"No. I know some place better."

Toyin looked down at their plates. "But we can't waste this food."

"We won't."

They took the food with them and ended up giving it to two very thankful homeless people.

"I'm still hungry," Toyin said as they left the happy pair.

"Be patient. It will be worth it."

He was right. She didn't know such savory culinary delights would be only a few blocks away. At first she hadn't been impressed by the décor of the small Japanese restaurant. It wasn't as luxurious as the hotel and they looked completely out of place in the casual atmosphere. But when the food arrived all her misgivings fell away as she enjoyed rich, chewy udon noodles shimmered in a savory miso broth the scent of garlic and sake wafting towards her, steam rising from every bite, fogging up her glasses.

Jackson stared at her, pleased by her expression of delight. "Am I right?"

"Absolutely worth it." She waved her hand. "Simple but heavenly."

"I noticed you drawing at the bar. Are you an artist?"

Heat touched her cheeks. She hadn't expected anyone to be watching her doing the silly sketch. It was an old habit. "Sort of."

"Sort of?"

"I used to draw comics until I realized there was no money in it. Now I own a pop-culture store called New Worlds and a startup called TJ Studios," she said with pride not knowing what she'd find out when she returned home.

"I'd like to see your work."

"Doesn't matter. I don't draw comics anymore."

"Why not?"

"Because it hurts too much. I briefly had a webcomic that failed miserably."

"So what? Start again."

"I was going to let the domain expire and—"

"Why would you do that? You already have a business making money, what's wrong with doing something else for fun?"

She didn't want to admit that she'd lost confidence in herself. "There are others so much better than me."

"Of course. That's how life works, but that doesn't mean you don't enter the ring. My stepfather is a boxing fan so forgive the reference."

"My work isn't the typical comic stories."

"Even better." He moved his chair next to her and handed her his phone. "Let me see it."

"What?" she said surprised by both his question and sudden closeness. She was flattered by his interest. "Right now?"

He nodded.

She went to her site and opened her archives.

He looked through it. "These are great. You shouldn't stop doing what you love."

Was he just being nice? She didn't want to think so. She liked talking about them. There were so few who believed in her. "I'm afraid to love anything anymore after Lance."

Jackson pointed to the screen. "This will never betray you."

"You sound like you understand."

He returned his seat back in place. "More than you know."

"I don't believe it."

He nodded. "It's true. A woman targeted me to destroy my family business. She ended up marrying my brother instead."

Toyin stared at him for a long moment, shocked. "And he doesn't know?"

"He knows now."

"And he doesn't care?"

"She doesn't want to destroy our family anymore."

"Are you sure?"

"Pretty much. We have a love-hate relationship. But she's not the first woman to use me…" And as she'd hoped he would he shared about the women from his past and the bad luck he'd had with them. They left the restaurant and went to a bar and he continued his tales. At first she didn't believe him, but as time passed and the drinks flowed she felt an affinity with him. He knew true heartbreak.

He spoke about his mother who'd passed around this time last year, but instead of being maudlin, he celebrated her life by sharing all that he loved about her, although Toyin could tell he missed her terribly. His mother sounded like someone she would have liked. She liked him too, surprised by how much, but he was easy to talk to. He made her laugh and she could make him laugh too in a way she felt he hadn't in awhile.

At times, he looked at her as if amazed by how funny she could be. She was amazed too. She'd never been able to make Lance laugh. And their shared laughter seemed to destroy any barrier between them. Jackson freely shared how baffled he was by the women he'd cared for and Toyin was baffled too. He seemed like a great guy. Why would he choose such awful women? *Unless he was a con man with a well scripted story,* a cynical voice whispered.

But then he did something—the slight movement of his head, the nonchalant way he lifted a shoulder in a shrug, she couldn't pinpoint what—that reminded her of someone she couldn't place— and her suspicions subsided. There was something genuine about him in spite of the flashy clothes and quick smile. She felt sorry for him. And for herself. Why did they have such bad luck?

"You need a bitch barometer," she finally said, feeling buzzed and angry.

"A what?"

"A way to measure whether a woman is a bitch."

He sighed. "First I'd need to find someone I could trust."

"We both could use someone like that."

The two left the bar and went to a club, at Jackson's insistence. Toyin didn't think any club would let them in because of her dress, but they didn't have any trouble and danced for an hour.

"It's been a great night," she said, feeling giddy from drink and dancing as she stopped in front of her hotel room. She hadn't gone dancing for a while and it had felt liberating. "You made me forget about Lance."

Jackson nodded. "But not enough," he said then pulled her into his arms and kissed her.

But not in a sloppy, drunken way she would have expected. He kissed her as if she were the only woman on earth; as if she were fine wine and he a sommelier. As if it had been a moment he'd been waiting for.

She'd never been kissed like that before—with both hunger and tenderness. Fire and velvet. Let alone by a man she'd just met. Toyin pulled away her heart thumping wildly, her skin hot. He left her breathless. Was that an invitation? Did he expect her to ask him to come inside? Did he just want to sleep with her? Had she misread him the entire time?

"Jackson—"

He rested his forehead against hers and whispered, "Marry me."

She paused. "What?"

"Marry me. Please."

"You're drunk."

He sighed. "Doesn't matter. I wouldn't ask you, if I didn't mean it. I need you."

"You need to sleep this off. Where's your room?"

He gathered her close and held her tight. "Please. I'll make it worth your while. You look so pretty."

"I look like a cadaver."

"A pretty one and you should be a bride and I need one. I need one to keep the others away. It won't be for keeps." He pulled something out of his pocket. "I even have a ring." He got down on one knee and opened the box. "See? I mean it. Please."

The diamond sparkled like a star that had fallen from the sky. "When did you get this?"

His eyes gleamed with hope. "Do you like it?"

"It's beautiful."

"It's yours."

"It costs a fortune."

He rested a hand on his chest and nodded. "That's right. I'm a Fortune."

"No, that's not what I said. Get up."

He shook his head. "We can get it resized if it doesn't fit. I've been carrying it around for a long time waiting for the right woman."

"Jackson, you don't know who I am."

"I do. And you know me too. And all night you never once asked me for something. I know that you won't use me. This is my idea not yours, right? You're not even sure about it. That's what makes you different. Others would jump at the chance."

She knelt in front of him. He didn't slur his words and his gait had been steady, but clearly he was intoxicated beyond reason. "Jackson—"

"I like you and you like me. It will be easy and quick. We go through the ceremony, take pictures for proof and then we get it annulled later." His eyes pleaded. "That's all I ask."

He was drunk, she was tipsy. She should have had more sense, but the idea was tempting. She wondered if the liquor had given his voice a sexy, husky edge or if it was just her imagination, no matter the reason she liked the sound of it. It stirred up desires within her.

To have a man, no matter what state he was in, ask her to marry him put her self-esteem back in place. Here was someone twice the man Lance was, a man who was way out of her league who she could use as proof that she wasn't a loser.

She saw a man and woman in casual dress send them curious glances as they walked down the carpeted hall. "They must have come from a costume party," she over-heard the man say.

Toyin jumped to her feet and opened her hotel door. She'd been a spectacle enough for the night. "Get up. We can talk inside."

He shuffled inside on his knees.

Toyin couldn't help a chuckle. "You look ridiculous."

"I feel ridiculous. Will you marry me or not?"

She closed the door behind him. "If I do, what happens after this? How do I contact you? I don't know where you live or—"

"Give me your cell phone. I'll give you my address when this is over. Just come by and say you're my wife. I'll take it from there."

"That does not sound like a well thought out plan."

He held out the ring. "Please. Save me from myself. You can keep the ring and later pawn it if you want. It's real."

Toyin took the ring and slid it on her finger. Surprised that it fit. "Okay."

Jackson jumped to his feet and kissed her. "You don't know how happy you've made me."

She stared at him for a moment, wondering if he was really as drunk as she'd suspected him to be. But he had to be because what he was asking was crazy. Why would he want to get married to her?

He took her hand and opened the door. "Come on. Let's go."

And soon after they were married. He kissed her on the cheek, took photos and acted like a jubilant groom, which made her laugh. She thought he would want to part ways after the ceremony but instead he said 'Let's pretend this is real' and they toured the city in a limo until dawn.

By the time morning came she took him back to his hotel, laughing at his halfhearted pleas to give him a real honeymoon, and did her best to forget the crazy night as she focused on her company and fought to keep her manager's betrayal from ruining her business.

Now Jackson was sober and he still wanted a bride and he could save her business. Love wasn't in the equation and that was perfect.

Chapter Eight

She'd said "yes".

Jackson pumped his fist in the air in victory. Toyin was still his. He'd avoided a disaster.

Reginald walked into the living room. "Is there something I should know?"

Jackson turned to him. "Know?"

"About Mrs. Fortune. Does she have special requirements?"

"We'll find that out later."

"I'd prefer to be prepared now. Should I get the room ready? Hire—"

"Do what you want to," Jackson said impatient and in no mood to think about details. "I'll play it by ear."

He only wanted to focus on the fact that she'd help him. He'd been afraid she may not continue to agree to this arrangement, but convincing her hadn't been as hard as he'd feared.

The doorbell rang.

Jackson sat down ready to deal with whoever it was. When Reginald opened the door an attractive woman with dark lashes and short brown hair stormed into the room past him.

Reginald shook his head and closed the door behind her. "Three women in one day, that must be a record for you."

She glared at Jackson.

He clasped his hands behind his head and smiled back at her. "Sylvia. This is a pleasant surprise."

"You are such a pig."

He blew her a kiss. "Feel better now?"

"No. Pig."

"Why is that?"

She folded her arms. "I thought we were friends."

"We are."

"We've even slept together."

He let his hands fall to his lap. "I know."

"And you get married without telling me?"

"Don't worry. I didn't tell anyone. It was a spur of the moment thing. I didn't tell my brother either."

"I thought you weren't going to see women for a while."

He shrugged. "I tried. I failed."

"You didn't try very hard." She pulled a face. "Why couldn't it have been me? I thought we were good together."

"We are. I didn't want to ruin a good thing."

She stood in front of him. "Is this for real?"

"Maybe."

"Why her?"

"I don't know." He lied. He knew very well why he'd chosen the woman sitting alone at the bar in a Corpse Bride wedding dress. He pretended to be a stranger, although he really wasn't, but Sylvia didn't need to know that. Nobody did, not even Toyin, until he was ready.

She rested her hands on her hips. "Are you really off the market?"

"For the time being."

Sylvia straddled his lap and sent him a knowing look. "Do you plan on being a good husband?"

"Yes," he said unable to ignore the soft feel of her bottom against him.

She unbuttoned her blouse. "How good?"

He removed her from his lap. "Very good."

She frowned and re-buttoned her shirt. "Pity." She laughed as a thought came to her. "Speaking of pity, you wouldn't believe what I saw coming up here. Some poor fat girl was helping this older woman who'd dropped her things in front of the elevator. Well, first her skirt ripped when she bent down then her wig got caught when the doors closed and was snatched right off her head. It was hilarious. You should have seen her face. I wish I had recorded it."

Jackson briefly closed his eyes and said in a tight voice, "She's not fat."

Sylvia sent him a strange look. "How do you know? You didn't see her."

"Was she wearing a black pencil skirt and blue blouse, fake lashes and a black wig with waves?"

Sylvia nodded. "But how did you—?"

"She's the new Mrs. Fortune."

"No, she's not."

Jackson nodded. "Yes, she is."

Sylvia pulled out her cell phone and glanced at the image of him with his new bride. "But she doesn't look anything like the photo online."

"She tried a makeover."

"It didn't work." When Jackson shot her a look Sylvia softened her criticism. "I mean I know she put in the effort, but the boxy look doesn't suit her and the makeup—"

"She'll learn."

"Poor Jackson. You must have been really drunk. There's no other way you would have ended up with someone like her."

He stood and shoved his hands in his pockets. "Want to get something to eat?"

"When do I get to meet her?"

"Soon, but she has to meet Edgar and Ava first."

"Together? Do you want to see her get eaten alive?"

He slipped on his socks and shoes. "I'll be there."

"It won't be enough."

He grabbed his coat and keys. "You shouldn't sound so hopeful."

"I'll try to behave myself. Oooh, poor girl."

"She's stronger than you think."

"At least I'm certain of one thing. I no longer need to be heartbroken."

Jackson opened the door for her. "Why not?"

"Because there's no way this marriage can last." She sauntered past him. "You'll come back to me."

Jackson smiled, but when she turned, his smile disappeared and he said in a low voice she couldn't hear, "Don't count on it."

Chapter Nine

"**I** heard about the elevator."

Toyin rested her head on her knees as she sat on the floor in her apartment. She almost wished she hadn't answered Jackson's phone call. She'd been in a fetal position for the past half hour remembering her embarrassment. She'd only just recovered. Now her face burned with renewed humiliation. How could he have found out? "Oh God, did someone record it? Is it online?"

"No," he said quickly. "A friend of mine saw you. I'm just making sure you're alright."

"The wig got destroyed along with my pride, but I'm fine."

"Good. I didn't ask if you needed help moving things in."

"No, I don't have much. Anything else?"

"Donate the skirt too, it doesn't suit you." He hung up."

Toyin made a face. "You didn't have to call if you were going to make me feel bad about it." But strangely, she didn't. He made her feel relieved. The outfit her sister had encouraged her to wear wasn't her at all. She went into the bathroom and scrubbed her face clean, took out her contacts, and put on her glasses then looked at her fresh bare face feeling better.

She was lucky that her parents and grandmother had traveled to see family in London and wouldn't be back for another week; otherwise her sister's fiasco would have been more of a disaster. Instead, their days would be so busy they wouldn't check online.

Toyin began to tidy up her apartment, tossing things in a laundry basket to wash before she packed them.

She was straightening her bed when she received a text from her sister.

Warning. Kemi's coming.

Why?

You know why.

This is all your fault.

Will you get paid?

Shut up.

She sighed. She heard her brother's footsteps outside her apartment before he pounded on the door. He was built like a truck with the fists to match. She counted to ten before she opened the door.

"What is the meaning of this?" he asked, storming inside.

He was three years her junior but because he was a male he acted like he was head of the household while their father was away. He had Maryam's coloring, but pointed features that made him look like a weasel when he was angry.

"Don't scrunch up your face like that," Toyin said. "You know it doesn't suit you."

"Don't change the subject." He took a deep breath. "Why didn't you tell anyone?"

"Because no one would understand."

"We thought you were with Lance."

"I did too, but he now belongs to someone else."

"Who is this man? When will we meet him? How did you—"

"When Mum and Dad return I'll explain everything. For now, just let them enjoy their travels and keep this quiet. My name wasn't mentioned so it shouldn't have spread far."

"It's spread far enough. Aunt Gretchen knows."

Toyin screamed.

Kemi covered his ears.

Toyin hand's trembled as she stared at him in horror. "How could she find out?"

"I don't know."

"If Maryam told her, I really will kill her."

"It won't help. She's on her way."

"Here?"

"Yes."

"Then why did you come?"

The doorbell rang and a weasel grin spread across his face. "Because I wanted to hear this," he said before he ducked into another room.

Chapter Ten

Aunt Gretchen and Cousin Tansy stood on the doorstep with identical big smiles. Their teeth beautifully white against their dark cocoa skin. Aunt Gretchen inherited Mama Bisi's commanding presence and handsome looks; her daughter Tansy was as cute as a kitten.

"My favorite niece," Aunt Gretchen said, kissing Toyin on both cheeks.

"My favorite cousin," Tansy said doing the same.

Aunt Gretchen took off her coat and handed it to Toyin. "I saw the news. You naughty girl! What a story. Your sister explained everything."

"What exactly did she explain?" Toyin asked, hanging up their coats.

Aunt Gretchen took a seat. "The details of how you met this wonderful man. We will have a big party and of course you know why we're here."

Toyin sat in front of them unsure. "Actually…"

"Oh, Mummy let me tell her," Tansy said, bouncing with excitement.

Aunt Gretchen shook her head. "I think it best that it comes from me."

"But it was my idea."

"What was your idea?" Toyin asked with growing dread.

The two women shared a look then said in unison, "A double wedding."

"What!"

"You didn't think you could get away with a simple elopement, did you?" Tansy said.

Aunt Gretchen nodded. "You have to have another wedding."

"And since I'm getting married Saturday—"

"Not this coming Saturday," her mother interjected.

"But the one after that," Tansy clarified. "I had this stupendous idea. Why don't we get married together?"

"That way you wouldn't have to worry about anything except the dress and arriving on time. I've already planned everything for my dear Tansy, it won't take much to add a few details for you."

"And we know all the same people."

"So no one will have to travel again to see you."

"And your parents are returning early. They'll call you when they get home. Your mother was upset—"

"Shattered," Tansy said with a sad shake of her head.

"—but I reassured her that all is well. To think you even thought of depriving your parents of this special moment is beyond me."

"But now you can remedy that."

Aunt Gretchen pressed her hands together. "There's one little problem."

"Only one?" Toyin said.

Her cousin nodded, not hearing Toyin's sarcasm. "You know it's our tradition that Mama Bisi chooses your match. She may be a teeny, tiny bit upset that you didn't include her in your choice."

"In other words she'll be completely put out, but," Aunt Gretchen said before Toyin could respond, "this wedding will show her that we're all standing behind you. You have to do this to keep the peace."

Tansy released a happy sigh. "Isn't it great? You're like a sister to me and we'll have the same anniversary."

They both stared at her.

Tansy nudged Aunt Gretchen. "Mummy, she's speech-less."

"I know. Give her time to process this."

"She looks like she's going to cry."

"I…I can't let you do this," Toyin managed to say. "It's too much and I don't think Jackson will—"

"Yes, the groom," Aunt Gretchen cut in. "We've thought of that. Your uncle is already prepared to talk to him to let him know how important this is to us. Where are his people from again?"

"I don't remember."

"Never mind. You can call me later and let me know."

"Why would you need to know that?" Toyin asked.

"The caterer can add one extra meal at cost, of course, but we don't want to exclude him from the festivities."

"This is really all too much and—"

"We've made an appointment to look at dresses tomorrow," Tansy said. "We have a tailor waiting to alter your dress so that it will be ready for the big day."

"Which is in less than a fortnight," Toyin said in a flat voice.

Tansy squealed with delight. "Yes. Isn't that marvelous? You won't get any presents, of course, but from what I heard he's loaded anyway so you won't want for anything…Mummy, she looks like she's going to cry again."

"Happy tears, my dear. Happy tears." Aunt Gretchen stood and kissed Toyin again. "You'll make a beautiful bride."

"We both will." Tansy kissed her also.

Toyin gave them their coats then waved goodbye.

Kemi popped out of the other room. "I heard there will be a live orchestra," he said with laughter in his voice.

Toyin closed the front door and spun around. She'd forgotten he was there. She pulled out her cell phone. "It's not funny."

"Who are you calling?"

"Maryam." When her sister picked up she said, "You have to fix this."

"Fix what?"

"Aunt Gretchen came by with Tansy and they're planning a double wedding."

"So what?"

"I can't go through this all over again."

"How much is he willing to pay you to get an annulment?"

Toyin glanced at her brother, she didn't want him to overhear. She walked to the kitchen and lowered her voice. "That's not the point."

"It's the entire point. How much?"

"Actually, he wants me to keep this up a little longer."

"Even better. How much?"

"It won't matter if he changes his mind."

"Why would he change his mind? You're already married. This is just an extra ceremony."

At times her sister's logic was aggravating. "In front of all our family and friends. It's a sham."

"No one needs to know that."

"I don't want another wedding. You started this. You have to talk to Aunt Gretchen and Tansy. Get them to change their minds."

"Oh sure," Maryam said with a laugh, "and while I'm at it I'll stop the sun from rising."

Toyin sighed. Her sister was right. There was no way to stop this disaster from happening.

Chapter Eleven

"Your wife is on the phone."

Jackson slowly opened his eyes. He glanced at the clock and saw it said eight-thirty. He groaned. It was Sunday morning and he'd hoped to sleep in until twelve. What cruel fate was this? "My what?"

"Wife," Reginald said. "Please don't pretend you don't have one. I'm not in the mood today."

Jackson slowly sat up and rubbed his eyes. "I wasn't pretending." He yawned. "What does she want?"

"That mystery can be easily solved by talking to her."

"Sarcasm doesn't suit you, Bo. She could have left a message."

"She's left three messages. All asking, or rather, imploring you to call her."

Jackson held out his hand. He didn't keep his cell phone in his bedroom, not wanting any devices that could interrupt his sleep. Reginald took the phone off mute and handed it to him before leaving.

"Next time call after ten," Jackson told her.

"This is urgent."

He yawned again. "Go on."

"We have a problem. A serious, horrible, terrible problem."

He rubbed his eyes. "Sounds bad."

"I'm not kidding."

"Go on."

"All yesterday I've been trying to fix it. I've called almost everyone I know to help me, but nobody can."

Jackson fell back on the bed, trying to stifle another yawn. "What's the problem?"

"My aunt and cousin are planning a double wedding. *Our* double wedding. They won't take 'no' for an answer. My parents are flying back early to help me prepare."

Jackson closed his eyes.

"Are you still there?" Toyin asked when he didn't reply.

"Yes, I'm waiting."

"Waiting for what?"

"The problem."

"I just told you the problem," Toyin said. "Weren't you listening?"

"Your aunt and parents are planning a wedding."

"No, my aunt and cousin are. My parents are coming back. Oh never mind. That's not the biggest issue. My cousin is planning to get married Saturday." She raised her voice to imitate Tansy's bubbly tone. "Not this coming Saturday, but the one after that." She returned her voice to normal. "Which means we have to get married again in front of everyone."

"Okay."

"Okay?!"

Jackson held the phone away from his ear and grimaced. "No need to shout."

"What is wrong with you? You're supposed to be outraged. You're supposed to say 'Are you joking?' 'Have you gone mad?' 'Is your family batty?' I have better things to do than plan another fake wedding."

"You just said your aunt is planning it. What else do we need to do?"

"In a couple hours they're dragging me to go dress shopping. You'll have to tell your family and friends, although my aunt did mention that there won't be enough room for too many more people."

Jackson put the phone on speaker, rested it on the bed and crawled back under the sheets. "It will be fine. I'll only add four more people."

"How can it be fine? How can we have this huge wedding and then break up in a couple months?"

"We'll stretch it to six."

"What was that? You sound far away."

He put his mouth closer to the phone. "We'll stretch it to six."

"What about my parents? They'll be devastated that—"

"We'll stay married for a year then."

Her voice cracked. "A year?"

"We go through the ceremony, make people happy then we separate. After several months the excitement should have worn off." He smiled pleased to have come up with such a solid solution so early in the morning. "Unless you have a better idea."

"No, I don't. You're handling this better than I thought you would."

"You don't know enough about me yet."

"I'm really sorry about this."

"Don't be. Just don't call me—"

"Before ten," Toyin finished. "I get it."

"Thanks." Jackson hung up and promptly fell back asleep.

Three hours later he wasn't as confident about his solution as he ate his breakfast. He should have thought about the possibility of another wedding. He always liked a party, but knew that this could complicate things. His family liked to do things a certain way. He knew they wouldn't take kindly to a surprise wedding they weren't in control of. Especially Edgar. He called James.

"I'm getting married again," he told him.

"What about Toyin?" his brother said alarmed.

"I'm getting married to her. Her family wants a wedding."

James started to laugh.

"They're planning it for next Saturday. In two weeks to be precise."

James laughed harder.

"I'm glad you find this so funny."

"More than you know."

"It's going to be a double wedding with her cousin."

"Are you making this up?"

"No."

"Does she have a large family?"

"I don't know that yet. I need a favor."

"Don't worry," James said. "We'll be there. Wouldn't miss it for the world. I'll take lots of pictures."

Jackson frowned. "That's not why I'm calling."

"What do you want?"

"I thought you should break the news to Edgar."

James's good humor disappeared. He swore. "I forgot I haven't told him yet."

"You can tell him now."

"Which part? That you're already married or that you're getting married again in two weeks?"

"Both."

"Why don't you tell him?"

"Because you say things better than I do."

"No," James said unmoved by the flattery, "it because you don't want to do it."

"That too."

"He'll want to meet her first," James said.

"There won't be enough time before the wedding."

"He'll make time."

Jackson nodded. "I know."

"And if he doesn't like her…"

"He won't have a choice. He'll have to."

"I'll see what I can do. I can manage to stall for a week and keep him in the dark. I'll let others know it's for the best considering his health. But after that, you'd both better be prepared."

"For what?"

James's tone turned ominous. "The summons."

Chapter Twelve

He never thought revenge would taste so sweet. James set his cell phone down and looked across the breakfast table at his wife, taking in her fine high cheekbones and exquisite dark skin. This morning she looked fetching in jeans and one of his blue sweaters. The remainder of their brunch— spinach and mushroom egg baked into a light pastry—sat on the table between them.

"What's the smile for?" Ava asked.

"We've been invited to a wedding."

"Whose?"

"Jackson's. He's getting married."

Her brows shot up. "Again?"

"It's to the same woman. Her family wants a formal wedding. Saturday. It's in two weeks. It's all arranged."

"Do you think he'll go through with it?"

"He'll have to."

Ava sent him a knowing look. "He's skipped out on weddings before."

"One wedding," James clarified. "And he was there…just not as the groom." He shook his head. "Water under the bridge. They're already married so it won't change anything."

"Except that it's a public declaration."

"Jackson likes the limelight."

"Does she?"

James frowned. "What woman doesn't want to be a bride?"

"That's not an answer."

"I don't know. If her family wants it, I'm sure she does too."

Ava's frown deepened. "It's not like you to apply fuzzy logic."

"I don't know her enough to form an opinion."

She playfully slid her foot up his leg and smiled. "That's better."

"You'll get to meet her soon, so you can tell me."

She rested her foot on his lap. "Do you believe him?"

He felt himself respond as she wiggled her toes against him. "About what?"

"That he planned all this. That he's tired of making mistakes with women and wants to use Toyin as a sort of shield?"

He covered her foot with his hand. "Right now I don't care what he does."

"James."

"If you want me to concentrate, you'll stop touching me like that."

Ava put her foot down. "Sorry." She winked. "You can punish me later."

James couldn't stop a grin. "With pleasure."

She took a sip of her orange juice. "Now about Jackson and Toyin."

James nodded, trying to refocus. "Yes. She's like no one he's ever dated before. He picked a good one. She found out that Enomwoyi was a fraud."

"You didn't tell me that."

James swore, he'd meant to keep it secret.

"When?" Ava pressed.

"That same morning. They happened to cross paths."

Ava made a pained expression. "Please don't tell me he was with another woman the same time Toyin showed up."

"I won't."

Ava closed her eyes and groaned.

"But she proved to me that she's not in it to use him. She said she loves him."

Ava stared at him. "So he's staying married?"

"Yes. I told you that."

Ava paused. "And you're not worried?"

"Why would I be worried?"

"Because this doesn't sound like Jackson at all."

"You don't know everything about my brother no matter how much you studied him. Besides, this is a good thing. It gives him the right image and keeps him out of trouble."

"What do you think he's up to?"

"I just told you."

"You don't mean that."

"I'm giving him the benefit of the doubt. You should too."

Ava chewed her lower lip. "What is she like? Professional? Beautiful?"

"No, she's pretty, but not beautiful."

"That's what you mean by saying she's different than the rest?"

James shook his head. "No, it's everything about her. I can't put my finger on it. Just trust me. She's good for him and she'll look out for him. Like I said, she discovered Enomwoyi was fraud, isn't that something?"

"Hmm."

"You don't sound impressed."

"That's like giving someone credit for chewing gum. I noticed her watching him at the charity party. It's no secret that your brother has terrible taste in women."

"Present company excluded of course."

Ava shook her head in disagreement. "No, not really. I could have done a lot of damage if I'd wanted to. He was…is easy to manipulate. We need to find out more about her."

"Why?"

"First I don't buy that those photos accidentally got posted. There was a calculated strategy behind them."

James thought for a moment before he shook his head. "But Toyin doesn't seem the type to—"

Ava held up her hand. "And their crazy elopement seems too coincidental. How can you possibly meet a stranger in Las Vegas, get married then discover that you live only twenty minutes from each other?"

James thought for a moment then said, "Few things are completely impossible. Statistically speaking you can argue that—"

"Improbable then."

He nodded. "Yes. You think she targeted him?"

"It's possible. *I* did."

James sighed. He wanted to be happy for his brother, but Ava had brought up a good point. What if Toyin wanted something? He liked her, but he didn't know her. "It could be nothing."

"I need to find out more about her. If we want to keep this family safe from your brother we—"

James clicked his tongue in pity. "You're forgetting something."

"What?"

"My brother was part of this family before you."

Ava had the grace to look embarrassed. "I didn't mean—"

"I know. You see the threats because you once were one, but you can relax. We look out for each other. I won't let him get hurt. He's not a threat and although his choices haven't been the best, he's a good man. We agreed that we'd give him another chance. Let's wait and see what Toyin's like. I'm going to talk to Edgar. I don't want you to do anything more. Don't go behind his back or mine."

"I wouldn't dare."

"Yes, you would."

She couldn't stop a tiny smile. "I'll try."

Chapter Thirteen

The smell of booze and spicy steak drafted towards him as Jackson sat in a private booth with his four friends that Friday night. His fraternity brothers. They'd put together a hasty post bachelor party as an excuse to get together and drink. Nearly a week had passed since Toyin had reentered his life.

"Man, I can't believe you really did this," Lee Chang said. He was a tall, thin guy who could consume more liquor than a man twice his size. He'd made enough money on bets in college to prove it. He lifted his nearly empty glass and shook his head. "You had us all fooled last time. And I saw this girl's picture, what were you thinking?"

Ari Stanz took a large bite of his steak and shook his head, running a hand over his buzzed hair cut. "Women like that are sometimes wildcats in bed. Am I wrong?"

"She's not his type at all," Jaleel Peterson said, stroking his beard, flashing the tattoo of a serpent on his wrist. "What the heck was she wearing?"

"She's the Corpse Bride," Jackson said.

"I think she's cute," Ari said.

Gary Holland gave a sad sigh as if the world were coming to an end. The heavyset man looked ten years older than the rest of them, although he was two years younger. "You shouldn't have married her. Your sex life is now officially over."

"Speak for yourself," Jaleel said. "I'm a happily married guy."

"Bet you're too scared of your wife to say anything else," Gary said." He sighed. "I am."

"What will we talk about if we can't talk about Jackson's women, right?" Lee said.

Ari nodded. "Even in college you could find the worst."

"At least they were all lookers. Remember those girls you got to come to our parties?"

For a moment the men were silent, lost in happy memories.

Lee nudged Jackson with his elbow. "Be honest. Edgar chose her, right?"

"I don't think Edgar would choose someone like her," Jaleel said.

Jackson just smiled. He didn't mind the insults; he hadn't married Toyin to impress anyone. He actually took pleasure in their disappointment. He didn't like being predictable and it would give people something to talk about. That was always a good thing.

"You cost me money," Gary said. "I bet you'd finally end up with Sylvia."

"We all did." Lee agreed.

Jaleel grinned, waving his wallet in triumph. "Except me."

Jackson shrugged.

Lee frowned. "What's wrong with you? You're quiet tonight."

"A man has a right to be depressed when his freedom ends," Gary said.

"Who wants to bet how long this will last?" Lee said.

The men laughed then placed their bets and enjoyed the food and drinks soon forgetting their uncharacteristically quiet friend.

Jackson looked around the room with little interest. His friends really didn't know him. No one did. He gave them the image they wanted because it was fun and worked…but recently he'd felt lost.

And angry.

Angry that he was a joke. A punch line. The one who got cheated on, dumped, used. Yes, the women were all beautiful, but that didn't matter. It still hurt. Toyin was the first person to listen to him. Really listen and not laugh. She seemed to understand that as funny as the stories may seem to others the pain was real. He didn't care what anyone thought of her because he didn't care what they thought of him.

He briefly closed his eyes knowing that was a lie. He did care, a little too much. He cared that Ava had wanted to see him suspended and that James had agreed.

He'd accepted that she was part of his—their—lives now and she'd made his mother happy, but he couldn't forgive her for trying to get him replaced, even briefly. He'd already lost too much. He couldn't let her take more from him. If he didn't have his job, what would he have left?

His brother's betrayal hurt. He knew James's logic but it wasn't enough. He should have stood up for him. No matter what.

Jackson remembered when he was nine and he'd gotten stung by a swarm of bees when he'd upset their nest trying to get a kite out of a tree. His mother had sighed as she tended his wounds and said, "You always get into trouble. *Why couldn't you be a little more like James?*" The expression on his face must have shown the hurt he felt by her statement because she quickly added, "But you're special the way you are." Unfortunately, her words came too late. Her careless words burned in his heart even now. *Why couldn't you be a little more like James?* Honorable James. Serious James. James didn't get into trouble, he fixed things. He was dependable. He didn't date women who only wanted something from him. He was the smart one.

Jackson was tired of being second best. Of being overshadowed. He watched Lee easily down another large glass to his friends' applause and absently wondered what Toyin was doing right now. He pulled out his cell phone and sent her a text.

Rescue me.

Why?

I'm bored.

So?

I want to see you

What are you doing now?

He looked around at his friends, feeling lonely. In the brief time he'd known her, he never felt that way with her. *Nothing.*

Where are you?

A club with my friends.

And you're bored?

Yeah.

Lonely?

He couldn't say yes, although he was glad she understood. He needed that, but he wouldn't admit it. *No, just bored.*

Want me to come get you?

His heart lifted. Yes. Yes. Yes! He wanted to be with the woman Sylvia called fat; who others didn't think was his type. He wanted to be with the pretty woman whose lips he couldn't get enough of, whose curves begged to be touched and felt perfect against him. He wanted to be with her and no one else. He gave her the address. *I'll be waiting outside.*

Chapter Fourteen

Why was she doing this? Toyin asked herself as she pulled her car up to the club. Its big, bright sign punctured the dark sky with neon blue and red lights.

Why had Jackson texted her and why had she felt the need to respond? What was she going to do with him? When she saw him standing outside the club bookmarked by two attractive women, her mood dipped even more. This was not how she wanted to spend her Friday night. It had been a tiring week.

She'd had to endure dress shopping (if it had been up to her it would have taken all of three minutes but with her aunt and cousin it had stretched to an hour and a half!), her parent's scolding, her aunt and mother gushing about the caterer's menu, plus dealing with the lies Shanna had told her lawyer as part of their upcoming case. Now she had to pick up a gorgeous man from a club because he was bored.

The money. She was doing this for the money. She'd already signed the contract Jackson (or James she wasn't sure) had created spelling out the deadline and termination clause, which included a detailed postnuptial agreement. Toyin had been happy to sign to prove she wasn't the greedy opportunist her sister had inadvertently made her out to be. After the contract was finalized, she was able to deposit enough funds to get a great lawyer who'd laid out a strategy to defeat Shanna's claims that she hadn't done anything wrong. Toyin watched Jackson laugh with the ladies and felt her heart constrict. She liked him more than she should. She sighed as she realized the real reason he'd texted her. He was tempted and she was his protection.

If he didn't have her, he'd likely take one—or both—of the beautiful ladies home with him and end up in another relationship that went nowhere.

But she was not going to get out of her car and approach him so that she could be exposed to the scrutiny of those women. She pulled out her cell phone and texted: *I'm here.*

She saw him look at his cell phone and glance around almost eager. She sniffed. He must really be tempted. He looked relieved she was there to stop him. When he looked past her, she rolled down the window and waved her hand. He smiled when he spotted her, said something to the two women that made them frown, then shoved his hands in his pockets and walked to her car.

He looked sad.

That surprised her. Only seconds ago he looked as if he was having the time of his life. Now he looked lost and lonely. Was he disappointed she'd shown up? Regretting that he wouldn't be with one of those women tonight?

Feeling trapped by their contract? By the upcoming wedding?

"What's wrong?" she asked him when he got into the passenger seat.

"Nothing," he said, flashing a grin and the brief sad expression on his face disappeared.

"It won't be forever."

"What?"

"This arrangement. In a couple months you can get back to doing what you usually do."

He frowned. "What are you talking about?"

"Never mind." Toyin started her car. "Where do you want to go?"

He rested his head back. "I don't care."

"Are you sure you're alright?"

He nodded then closed his eyes.

But she didn't believe his casual attitude. Something was bothering him. Was he having regrets? Was the madness of the charade finally hitting him? He had seemed too casual on the phone the other day and she hadn't spoken to him for almost a week. Maybe the magnitude of everything had hit him. In a couple of days they had to perform this farce in front of everyone.

"I'm really sorry about the wedding," she said.

"It's okay."

He was quiet on the ride and she didn't want to bother him but he was a hard man to ignore. She felt self-conscious about every aspect of him. Of course it was hard to ignore a man in a green and gold suit. How come he managed to look good in anything no matter the combination? Why did she wish she could loosen his tie…no, take it off completely so that she could use it as a blindfold. Yes, she thought, her pulse picking up speed. She'd blindfold him while she slowly stripped him down, layer by layer until she exposed his smooth brown skin and had a chance to find out if his underwear was as colorful as everything else he wore. And then she'd pull it down and fall on her knees and capture him in her mouth. Then she'd suck him like a big chocolate bar…

Toyin shook her head, her body tense and hot. That was not why she was here. She was supposed to protect him. Not want him, even though she did. So much so she was tempted to pull the car over and jump him. She already knew what it was like to kiss him (delicious), to have him hold her close (heavenly), but there was still so much more to learn. And she'd be a willing student.

Toyin groaned and softly swore. She had to get a hold of herself. She turned the car into the parking lot, happy to have reached their destination. Jackson Fortune had to remain off-limits. "Okay," she said a little louder than she'd planned. "Here we are."

Jackson opened his eyes and looked around. "Where?"

"New Worlds. My store. I've got some inventory I want to go through then I'll drop you home. Unless you wanted to go somewhere else," she added when he hesitated.

"No, this is fine."

Her grandmother made her office feel like a cramped pantry; Jackson made it feel like a bathtub. She'd briefly taken Jackson upstairs to show him where she had TJ Studios, sharing that she'd been relieved the landlord hadn't raised her rent, before taking him to her office in the back of the store. The space had never felt so small before and every time she moved she felt as if she were bumping into him. "Excuse me," she said for what seemed like the thousandth time when she had to pass by him to grab something from the shelf.

"Who's that?" Jackson asked, pointing to a black and white photo on her wall.

"Jackie Ormes, the creator of the Torchy Brown comic. The first African-American female cartoonist." She motioned to the image of the woman beside her. "Most people know Barbara Brandon as the first nationally syndicated cartoonist, but Ms. Ormes' work was in newspapers years before her." She pointed to two more images of attractive older white women. "And that's Jacky Fleming and Lynn

Johnson. Those are names people know but there are lots of women in comics who people don't know."

"Which is why you have New Worlds."

"One reason. I wanted to make a living off of my love of art and pop-culture."

Jackson nodded then picked up a small booklet peeking from underneath her desk. He flipped through it. "What's this?"

Toyin looked at the item and smiled. "I'd wondered where that had disappeared to! It's something I'd done for 24-hour comic."

"What's that?"

"It's a challenge to create a twenty-four page comic in twenty-four hours. We hosted an event here last year and had ten participants. I've tried it four times and the fifth time I finally made it. That is one of my failures."

Jackson started to read the story about three African princesses on the hunt of a mystical medallion. "Why is it a failure? It looks good to me."

"But I didn't finish it by the deadline."

"So what? You can still finish it. I'd like to know what happens."

"I don't have the time. I don't draw comics anymore unless it's for challenges like that. I used to draw them all the time." She didn't tell him that while other kids babysat for money, she had started selling her work at fifteen to a website that nurtured and encouraged the creation of comics by girls. "At eight I fell in love with the watercolor illustrations of Pokémon. But as an illustrator you make much more money doing something else."

Jackson turned another page of the comic. "When did you start drawing?"

"Since I can remember." She hesitated, eager to share more but unsure. Because he wasn't looking at her she felt a little more confident, she took a deep breath before she said in a rush, "I used to tape and freeze frame the cartoon *Pinky and the Brain* so that I could draw them."

Jackson continued to keep his head lowered and nodded in understanding. "That's one smart kid."

Toyin felt her tension ebb, pleased he didn't think she was weird. Surprised he knew the characters she was talking about. Then she remembered the graphic novel she'd been reading at his apartment. "And I used to do the same with the films by Hayao Miyazaki. As a teenager I dreamt of getting the Kim Yale Award for Best New Female Talent by the Friends of Lulu." A sad smile touched her lips. "Never did and never will."

"You could still finish this," Jackson said, nodding to the unfinished comic book. "I'll buy it." He lifted his gaze to hers. "Consider it a commission."

"You're serious?"

He sent her a look.

She sighed. "I know. When it comes to money you're always serious."

He smiled.

"Must be nice to have money."

"It is. You have a week."

She stared at him for a moment then shook her head. "No can do."

"Why not?"

"I'm getting married this weekend."

Jackson laughed. "That's right. I can't believe a week has already passed. Two weeks then."

"I'm amazed you forgot."

He shrugged then said with a big grin, "One day I'm going to get you to draw me."

She looked at him and that strange sense of familiarity gripped her again. But this time she made the connection. He reminded her of a boy named Jacky she used to know. She couldn't understand why he had her thinking about a boy from so long ago. A boy she hadn't thought of in years. She'd thought she'd forgotten him. She'd only been six at the time, but he'd made an impression. She remembered how he would always come around her. It used to annoy her at first. He was always bouncing around, the teacher scolding him because he'd jump out of his seat and had a hard time staying still.

"Wow!" he said when he caught her drawing during play time. "You can really draw. Draw me. Draw me." He held out his arms and struck a pose. "I'm really strong."

"I don't want to."

"Please. Please."

"No."

His arms fell to his side. "Do you want to be my girl-friend?"

"No. You have three. My mom says you can only have one."

He shrugged. "I like them all and they like me."

He was right. Jacky and his three girlfriends were always sitting together at lunch time. Most people liked him. Even the teacher. But Mrs. Lorquette hated her. Toyin feared her. She always seemed to choose her when she didn't know the answer. She once caught Toyin sketching an answer to one of her questions and had ripped the sketch from her and said, "You're supposed to be paying attention."

"I was…that's my…"

"I don't care. You're to behave as everyone else does."

She hated going to school. When everyone else had their hand up to respond to a question she could feel Mrs. Lorquette's gaze land on her. "Toyin, what is the answer?"

She hung her head feeling stupid.

"I know, I know," Jacky said, waving his hand and bouncing in his seat. "It's—"

Mrs. Lorquette frowned, but her tone was patient and soft. "Jacky, it's not your turn. I didn't ask you."

"But Toyin told me the answer," he said pointing to her drawing. "That's how I know it." Then he gave the proper answer and the matter of her drawing pictures during class was settled. For one day at least. School was still awful for her because she was a child who expressed herself better with gestures and pictures than with words.

She still found Jacky annoying but as a thank you for that day, she drew him on an elephant. Elephants were her favorite animal to draw. She remembered his bright smile when she gave it to him.

She looked at Jackson now, that boy's smile lingering in her thoughts. "It's strange," she said. "But when you smile like that I feel as if I know you from somewhere."

"Really?" he said, sounding bored. He left the office and his disinterest wiped Toyin's nostalgia from her mind.

She finished her inventory check then locked up the office and watched Jackson stroll around the empty store. "You have a great place here," he said. "Do husbands get discounts?"

She didn't know why the mention of the word "husband" affected her but it did. He was her husband. She had a husband. A sexy, gorgeous husband who liked her drawings. How had that happened?

"Yes. Five percent."

"Fifteen."

"Okay, ten."

"Fifteen."

She threw her hands in the air. "Will you ever let me win a negotiation?"

"Fifteen."

She grabbed a bag from the food display in front of the cash register. "Ten and I'll throw in coconut chips."

Jackson took the bag and opened it. "Fifteen."

"Fine."

He kissed her cheek. "Thanks, honey."

Toyin touched her cheek, feeling oddly moved. "You're good at this."

"At what?"

"Pretending we're married."

He tossed some chips in his mouth. "We are married."

"That it's real."

He nodded. "By the way you're on the clock."

She frowned. "Clock?"

"If you wanted to say that special phrase to me."

Toyin searched her mind then remembered that he'd pay her for telling him she loved him. "Nobody's listening."

"I'm listening."

"It's not the same. You don't need a woman to tell you she loves you in private."

Jackson looked at a display of collectibles. A brief sad expression crossed his face again before he pointed to one of the objects and said, "How much?"

"What happened?"

He kept his gaze on a premium Batman statue before shifting to look at Rey and BB-8 from Star Wars. "Nothing."

She walked over to him, cupped his chin and forced him to face her. "I love you. Feel better now?"

He grinned, desire lighting his eyes. "A little."

She swallowed hard and turned to head back to her office to double check that she'd locked it. "You're a strange man."

Jackson stopped her, wrapping his arms around her waist. "Thanks for rescuing me," he whispered, his breath warm against her ear.

A delicious shiver coursed through her. "I didn't do anything."

"You came back into my life when I needed you most."

"How much have you had to drink?"

He turned her to him, his eyes studying hers with curious intensity. "Las Vegas wasn't a mistake."

She laughed, trying her best not to feel hypnotized by him. Desperate not to fall under his spell. "You believe in destiny?"

"Toyin—"

"I wasn't going to tell you but a pretty woman who walked like a cop stopped by."

His expression grew guarded. "Sylvia. What did she want?"

"She said she wanted to meet me." Toyin lowered her gaze, her voice faltering. "She let me know that you two are *very* close."

"Not as close as she wants us to be. She's not one of the ones who broke my heart." Jackson touched her cheek with a tenderness that had her craving more. "Still thinking about Lance?"

Toyin blinked, surprised by the question. "Not as much as I used to."

"I can help you forget him completely," he said, his words a velvet promise.

She knew what he was offering. A night with him. A night she wanted. This was why she'd answered his text. Why she'd come to see him.

Her cell phone rang, breaking the spell.

"I'm sorry," Toyin said, checking the number. "I have to get this."

Jackson smiled. "It's okay. I'm very patient."

Chapter Fifteen

Edgar Fortune used to only dream of ambition. Now his dreams were filled with her. His darling wife Flo. At times he wondered when the pain of loss would ease, but other times he feared that it would because his longing made him feel alive. His pain made his love for her feel even sweeter than it had felt when she was by his side.

"Edgar?"

He opened his eyes at the sound of his stepson's voice. He hated feeling weak. The health scare last week had been an embarrassment, but after a few tests he was sent home and told to rest. For the past several days people had tiptoed around him as if they expected him to break. It had been annoying. He sat up in his bed. He'd rested his head for a nap that had lasted longer than he'd meant it to.

The sun sat lower in the sky, signaling that Saturday evening was closing in. He hadn't been as productive as he'd hoped to be but planned to be back in the office Monday. He looked at his stepson's dark trousers and dark green shirt and knew he was talking to James. "What is it?" He held up his hand. "And don't ask me how I am. I'm fine. I gave you a little scare to keep you on your toes. I'm not planning to go anywhere yet. Even if I tried, I'm sure your mother would send me back to finish what I started."

"Yes, well…there's been a development."

"What kind?" He swung his legs over the side of the bed and grabbed a cigar from his cigar box. "Has something happened?"

"The business is fine as always," James said, guessing his concern. "It's Jackson. He's…getting married."

"Married? Did you say married?"

"Yes, the wedding is this Saturday."

"Today? How can you—"

"No, this coming Saturday."

"To who? Where? Who's arranging it?"

"Her family."

"Why haven't I heard anything about her before? Can we delay it in any way?"

"No, there's no point. They're already married. This is just a formality."

Edgar rolled the cigar between his thumb and forefinger, agitated. "Already married?"

"It was quick and from what he told me, was sort of whirlwind."

"Your brother picked up a bad habit from you and Ava," Edgar said referring to their own wedding last year when James had eloped with Ava to Vegas.

James rubbed the back of his neck. "It's not quite the same."

"How long have you known?" He crumbled the cigar in his hand. "Why wasn't I told sooner?"

"We weren't sure—"

Edgar let the ruined cigar fall to the ground and wiped his hands. "This is a disaster."

"No, she's good for him. A good influence."

James's cool tone helped ease some of Edgar's anxiety. "What is she like? What does she do? Dear God, please tell me she's not a stripper."

"Jackson has never dated a stripper."

"But that woman with the blondish hair and tight—"

"Was a dentist."

Edgar sniffed. "She didn't look like any dentist I've seen before."

"Things change," James said simply.

Edgar shook his head. "Your mother and I had someone we'd hoped…but that doesn't matter now. What do you know about her?"

"She's the middle child of three and attended the—"

Edgar waved his hand impatient. "Don't care."

"She's pretty. An artist."

"She's an artist? What's the use of an artist in the family?"

"She also owns a comic and pop-culture shop and a separate startup called TJ Studios so she's business minded."

"How business minded can she be with a comic book shop? What is that anyway?" He continued before James could reply, "Why have something like that when people can buy what they need online? Aren't bookstores dying like flies? Why would a niche store like that survive? It doesn't sound as if she has much sense."

"Her business is doing very well. She has a solid online presence."

"Hm…you also mentioned Something Studios. How is that going?"

"It's still growing."

"Which means she's struggling. Probably needs someone else to keep her afloat. I've warned you two about women like that. Never get caught by a woman who wants to get her hands on your willy and your wallet."

"I don't think—"

"You know what your brother is like. This woman could suck him dry. Have you looked at the prenup?"

James cleared his throat and made a noncommittal sound.

"Make sure you do. I'm depending on you. We can't let ourselves become vulnerable to anyone. I want to meet her."

"She's busy with the wedding planning so—"

Edgar sent him a hard look. "I don't care. Make it happen. Now."

Chapter Sixteen

Thursday.

His brother hadn't been able to delay the meeting with Edgar any further than that.

"It's close enough to the wedding day to rein him in," James explained. Jackson had thanked him for the help then told Toyin the news. She tried to come up with alternative dates that he patiently countered until she finally agreed.

He heard the nervousness in her voice, but felt rejuvenated. He'd regained the trust of his team at work after his latest missteps and ideas filled his mind. He'd met the week with a focus and vigor he hadn't felt in a while. If getting married made a man feel this way, he was ready for more. Sylvia had discovered how much when he'd invited her out for drinks the Saturday night after his Friday post bachelor party.

"I heard you met Toyin," he said in a neutral voice as she finished her martini and ordered another.

She stared at him as if she'd been caught stealing. "I was in the neighborhood and wanted to see what her store was like."

Jackson rested his chin in his hand and continued to study her. "I find threats boring, don't you?"

"I wasn't trying to…" She began but Jackson's unwavering stare made the words die on her lips. "I'm sorry. I was curious. I couldn't believe…" She sighed. "I'll leave her alone."

He smiled. "Good girl."

Sylvia traced the base of her glass with her finger. "She was nice and looked much better this time. Pretty." A reluctant, knowing smile spread on her face. "But you don't care what I think, do you?"

His smile remained.

"You don't care what any of us think." When he again didn't reply she nodded in resignation. "I guess I need this more than you." She raised her second glass. "To friends."

He touched her glass with his and softened her disappointment with a wink. "Always."

The next day he sent her flowers. That Tuesday he returned home ready to go over some marketing plans when Reginald opened the door as he was about to open it.

"There's someone here to see you," he said.

Jackson handed him his coat and keys. "Who?"

"She's waiting in the living room."

"And you let her in because…?"

"She'll explain herself." He turned.

Jackson walked in and saw a tall older woman sitting as still as a statue. "Hello, I—"

"I am called Mama Bisi. Forgive the intrusion," she said in a clipped English tone. "Please sit."

Jackson did, not daring to refuse her.

"I wanted to talk to you about my granddaughter Toyin."

He nodded.

"She must never know I came to see you."

He nodded again.

Her dark eyes studied him for a moment then she sat back and sighed. "It won't do. She is no good for you and I say this out of love for her." She pointed a finger at him, her long red nail fashioned like the tip of a sword. "You have the eyes of a fox and the heart of an elephant. It is steady and true. Such a contradiction will cause you pain because most people won't see it. Yes, I can see by your eyes that I am right. No woman has been worthy of your heart yet. Yet you give it out freely. Too freely."

Jackson cleared his throat, uncomfortable. "Madam, I—"

"Is your mother still living?"

"No."

"Yes, so you're even more vulnerable. Take heed of this warning. You do not want a woman who has the heart of a dragonfly. It cannot hold tight to someone who cannot rest in one place. Do not continue with her."

Jackson fell silent a moment before he said, "And if I do?"

She narrowed her eyes. "I see the fox is stubborn and a little selfish too." She stood. "I can only warn you."

"Why not tell me how?"

She looked at him surprised. "How?"

"How to win her heart."

Mama Bisi shook her head. "You can't without sacrificing your own."

Chapter Seventeen

She couldn't escape.

Jackson's call had stunned her. His stepfather wanted to meet her before the wedding—at all costs. She'd tried to tell him that her week was busy—coming up with false excuses—but nothing worked. Thursday was D-day. It wasn't fair. Jackson had managed not to meet her family yet, why couldn't she have been as lucky? The closer she got to her wedding day the less she thought she had any good luck at all.

But she couldn't escape it. Her first impression had to be good.

Toyin emerged from her bedroom with her hair pulled back wearing a simple white and black dress. Jackson would soon pick her up.

Maryam frowned. She'd stopped by to offer advice and support. "You look like a nun. No, a novice."

"It's not funny."

"Which is why I'm not laughing. You're not attending a funeral."

It feels like it. "I'm trying to look sophisticated."

Maryam went to Toyin's closet and pulled out a patterned dress with a West African flair and European accent. Toyin briefly smiled picturing Jackson in a matching suit.

He would love the bold yellow, red, green and orange colors. But would his stepfather? Could she take the risk?

She shook her head and adjusted her glasses. "It's too much."

"It's perfect. Besides, you don't have much time."

Toyin took the dress. At least she knew Jackson would be pleased. She wondered what combination he'd show up in. Metallic silver with purple accents? Plush mauve? She changed into the dress. "I'm only in this mess because of you."

Maryam rested a hand on her hip, unapologetic. "You're married to a wealthy man. You're going to have a big wedding, where's the mess in that?"

"Now I have to lie to his family."

Maryam grabbed Toyin's cheeks and spread her lips into a forced expression. "Just do it with a smile."

"I hope you don't mind—" Toyin began when she opened her front door. But the words died on her lips. She hadn't expected to see James. He wore a dark suit and blank expression. "Oh, I thought Jackson was picking me up."

He nodded. "He is."

"Where is he?"

"You're looking at him."

She looked at Jackson's somber suit. "What happened to you?"

"I want to annoy my sister-in-law. Don't worry, it won't last."

Toyin glanced down dismayed. "But I can't go dressed like this. We look completely different. I—"

He pressed his lips against hers in a feather light kiss. "Look perfectly beautiful."

The way he said it she almost believed him. "I can still change." She heard a loud cough. "Oh," she said turning. "This is my older sister, Maryam. The cause of all this mayhem and—"

"Nice to finally meet you," Maryam interrupted, holding out her hand. "You look better in person."

Toyin grabbed her purse and coat not trusting the look in her sister's eyes. "We're leaving now. No, first I have to change."

"No," Jackson and Maryam said in unison.

"Listen to your sister," he said.

"Listen to your husband," she said.

Toyin glared at them both then pointed at her sister. "I will get you back for this one day." She pointed at Jackson. "And you—" She looked him up and down at a loss for words. "Never mind. Let's go."

"Have fun," Maryam called out in a singsong voice as Toyin closed the door.

"What should I expect?" Toyin asked as they walked to Jackson's red Porsche. "What's your sister-in-law like?"

"Depends on who you ask. To my brother, she's a dream. To me a nightmare."

Chapter Eighteen

J ackson never knew shock could be such a beautiful expression. He enjoyed the look on both James and Ava's faces when he walked into the great room of the family home.

"Toyin," Jackson said. "You've already met my brother, James and the frozen witch, I mean wife, by his side is Ava."

"A pleasure," Toyin said.

"What game are you playing?" Ava asked him.

He shot her a look. "One I plan to win." He looked at James. "Where's Dad?"

"He'll be down soon."

"I'm here right now," Edgar said, displaying no sign of illness. He was a man of average height with a thick, muscular build and skin the color of roasted almonds and looked ready to take on the world. He patted Jackson on the back. "I looked over the report thanks, James."

"You're welcome," James said from across the room.

Edgar frowned and looked up at Jackson then looked at James. "Wait," he stumbled over to a chair and sat down. "I think I may be suffering a stroke."

"It's not you, Edgar," Ava said. "It's one of Jackson's childish pranks."

Jackson grinned. "Speaking of pranks…kidnapped any-one lately?"

"I said I was sorry."

"I thought you meant it until you tried to get me fired."

"I never said that. I only—"

"Why don't we all sit down to dinner?" James said.

"Where's Rudy?" Jackson asked, referring to his younger brother Rudolph. "I'd hoped Toyin would get a chance to meet him."

"At a friend's house," Edgar said. "He'll meet Toyin at the wedding."

"We wouldn't want him getting too attached to some-one who may not be around long," Ava said under her breath.

In the dining room Edgar took his place at the head of the table briefly looking over the couscous-stuffed green and yellow peppers in the center of the table before he looked at his two stepsons. He frowned. "One of you take off your jacket or something. It's disturbing to see you two looking so similar."

"Oh, give it time Edgar," Ava said. "You'll soon notice the difference. Jackson could never replace his brother."

"No," Toyin said, sensing Jackson stiffen beside her. She covered his hand. "I'm not in love with James."

"True," Ava allowed, "but some may wonder if you're really in love with Jackson."

Jackson shoved his chair back ready to stand.

Toyin squeezed his hand, stopping him. "No, it's okay. I expected your family to be suspicious of me. You haven't had the cleanest record with women after all. She's only looking out for you."

Ava nodded. "I'm glad you understand."

"Completely." She patted Jackson's hand. "And I'm not going anywhere soon. So we'll get a chance to get to know each other."

"I'd like that."

"We're not the easiest bunch to know," Edgar said. "What do you do Tonya?"

"It's Toyin."

He nodded. "What do you do?"

James cleared his throat. "I told you she—"

"I know what you told me," Edgar cut in with a hard look. "I want to hear her say it."

"I own a store called New Worlds and another business called TJ Studios," Toyin said.

"Profitable?"

"One more than the other."

"That will have to change. You're a Fortune now. If one of us fail we all fail. We'll have someone look over your financials."

Toyin shifted in her seat, uncomfortable. "That's not necessary."

"Of course it's necessary."

"Jackson is already helping me with my legal fees."

"Legal? Are you being sued?"

"No," Jackson said. "One of her employees stole from her. She's working with Moore's firm."

Edgar grinned. "Excellent. She'll crush this person like a maggot." He rubbed his hands together. "You'll soon learn not to turn your back on your business. You can't be too nice or too careful." He looked at Jackson. "I'm glad you've decided to settle down. I was getting worried about you and you know I hate worrying about anything."

"We have a new campaign rolling out soon."

"Hope it won't be as costly as the new logo launch."

"It won't."

Edgar shifted his gaze between Toyin and Jackson. "She even dresses like you when you're not trying to confuse me. She's as colorful as a piñata," he said with a laugh. "A shame your mother couldn't see this."

"I think Flo would see right through it," Ava mumbled.

Jackson glared at her.

She winced when her husband kicked her. "What? We're all thinking it."

"Thinking what?" Edgar said.

"Nothing," Jackson said.

Ava looked at Toyin then glanced at her hand covering Jackson's. "You don't have to try so hard. No matter what this really is we're all willing to accept it."

Toyin looked around the table not knowing what to say. She felt exposed as a fraud. Like a big red tomato in a barrel of peanuts. But then she remembered him sharing what Ava had done to him, how this marriage would protect his position at the company. So for his sake she wanted to stand strong. She would show Ava that she wasn't a push-over and that Jackson wasn't the man she believed him to be.

Toyin took a deep breath and thought of a moment when she was ten and had handed in a book report using only pictures. She'd been proud of it, but her teacher had given her an F for not following instructions. She recalled that pain now and let her eyes fill with tears.

She stared at Ava, making her voice shake. "Yes, you're right. You all know that I'm fooling myself." She brushed away a tear. "This is all too wonderful to believe and I know that Jackson could never love me as I love him. Even though he's loved many other women, including you. Excuse me." She jumped to her feet and raced out of the room.

She left them all in silence.

"What the hell just happened?" Edgar finally asked.

James turned to Ava. "Why did you have to push it?"

"I didn't think I'd make her cry." She glared at Jackson. "What did you tell her about me?"

"Enough," Jackson said. "Although I never told her I loved you."

James rested his napkin on the table. "Aren't you going to go after her?"

"I'm sure she went to the powder room."

"Assuming she knows where it is." James stood. "I'll go find her."

"No," Jackson said standing. "I will." He glared at Ava. "And when I get back you'll apologize."

She didn't want to go back.

Toyin rested her head against the wall in the hallway and closed her eyes. It was too much. Edgar talking about killer lawyers. Ava wearing a black suit that could easily cost several thousand dollars. They lived in a mansion. What was she doing? She felt like an actress lost in a melodrama. *I'm fooling myself that he'll ever love me?* Who says that in real life? They'll know she's a fraud. Especially Ava. Beautiful, smart Ava. She shouldn't have tried to pretend she could defeat her.

"Hey!" Jackson said in a loud whisper. "What are you doing?"

"Hiding. That woman scares me."

He held her shoulders then cupped her face, his eyes searching hers. "Did she really make you cry?"

"No." She sniffed in derision. "I just remembered a bad memory."

"You're doing great."

"Nobody believes a word I'm saying."

"Yes, they do. James is really upset Ava made you cry. I think she'll leave you alone from now on."

"I hope so." Toyin shivered. "Sitting in front of those two is creepy. She has eyes like laser beams and his are no better. I feel like I've been abducted and being analyzed by aliens who have taken human form."

Jackson laughed. "I understand the feeling but they're really not that bad, at least James isn't and…Ava has her moments."

"She reminds me of someone. Is she *really* the one you nearly married?"

"Trust me. She wasn't like this when we were dating. It was later that I started to get suspicious."

"She's really beautiful."

"Brilliant too, but I never slept with her."

"I didn't ask."

"But you were wondering."

She looked down.

He rested his hand against the wall behind her head. "You're making this look easy."

She lifted her gaze to his, startled. "What?"

"Being in love with me."

"If—" Toyin stopped when she heard footsteps, but she lost her breath completely when Jackson pulled her close and covered her mouth with his in a wild, hot kiss.

James stopped short. "Oh, I wondered what was taking you two so long."

Jackson waved him away. "We'll be there in a minute."

James laughed. "Take your time."

Once he was out of hearing, Toyin pulled away, breathless. Her body felt heavy and warm. "Why did you—?"

"You know why," Jackson said in a deep, husky voice before he pressed his open lips to hers once more.

After a few more seconds of shimmering, burning pleasure, Toyin reluctantly drew back. "Nobody is watching now. We have to go back."

A sly grin touched his lips. "You heard my brother. We can take our time."

"That's just a saying. He didn't mean it."

He kissed her neck, letting his hand slide down her side. "I do."

She ducked away and headed down the hall. She didn't want to go back, but being alone with him was far more dangerous. "Come on. If you're right, the rest of dinner should be a breeze."

Chapter Nineteen

"I know her from somewhere," Ava said as she sat beside her husband in the great room after their guests had left. Edgar had retired to his room.

"Probably because you saw her picture," James said.

Ava shook her head. "No, it's not that."

"I'm relieved that he finally found someone who loves him more than he loves her."

"You really think she loves him?"

James threw his head back amazed. "Why are you being so suspicious? You met her. You made her cry."

"I know, but I have this feeling that I'm missing something important."

He kissed her forehead. "Put away your knives. You did enough damage today."

Ava sighed with remorse. "I didn't mean to hurt her feelings. She really was a shock. She's not at all what I expected." Ava hit him in the stomach. "You should have warned me."

James rubbed where she'd hit him and said in a wounded voice. "She shocked me too. She didn't look like that when I first met her. Her hair was longer and her eyes seemed bigger somehow and the clothes were more…uh…different."

"Not his type at all."

"She draws and likes comics. They probably fell in love over manga."

Ava sat up and clapped her hands. "That's it! Why didn't I think of it before? The comic shop! New Worlds…of course. It was staring me right in the face. It's her! That's where I've seen her. I haven't gone there in awhile, but when I was seeing Jackson I once took him there." Ava sat back pleased by the connection and remembered that spring day and how he'd behaved.

He'd been mildly impressed by the décor when she'd told him about the popular store that catered to women. She had left him to wander around so that she could look at a selection of graphic novels when she heard the sound of a display crashing to the ground. She turned and saw Jackson quickly trying to right it as well as the magazines that had been scattered on the floor. "I'm sorry," he said in a frazzled manner she'd never seen before. "I…I didn't see it."

"What happened?" Ava asked staring at the mess.

Jackson didn't reply as he fell on his knees and quickly gathered the magazines. A pretty woman in a silver wig, dark framed glasses, wearing a yellow shirt with the store logo on it, came up to them. Before she could speak, Ava said, "I apologize on my boyfriend's behalf. Maybe you should ban men entirely."

"No," the woman said with a laugh. "It's okay. At least it wasn't the collectible display case. I'll take care of it. Is there anything you were looking for? I could—?"

Jackson jumped to his feet, keeping his gaze lowered. "No, I'm fine. Thanks." He turned to Ava. "I'll meet you outside." He held out his hand. "Give me the keys, I'll wait in the car."

Ava gave him the keys. "I'll just—"

He snatched the keys and turned. "No rush. Take your time."

Ava watched him hurry out of the store confused. "He's not usually like that."

"He looked really embarrassed," the woman said as they both watched him jump into Ava's car like a storm was chasing him.

Ava agreed. That wasn't like Jackson either. Few things embarrassed him. He usually had a smile, laugh or joke to cover any awkward occasion. She didn't think too much about it as she had her items rung up.

She returned to the car where she found Jackson with his head on the dashboard. She handed him a magazine. "The woman you met was the owner and she says no hard feelings. She hopes you feel comfortable coming back. She thought you might like this. It's a comic she published."

Jackson barely glanced at the magazine before he tossed it in the backseat. "Thanks."

Ava turned to reach for the discarded item, offended. "If you don't want it—"

He stopped her, grabbing her arm. "I do…I just…" He took the magazine, rolled it up and tucked it inside his jacket. "I'll look at it later."

Ava chewed her lip as she thought about that forgotten incident. She'd figured that Jackson had been so overwhelmed by the décor that he hadn't paid attention, he did things like that, but now she wondered if it had been Toyin instead. "I think he knows her."

"Maybe. Jackson knows a lot of people."

"Yes, and I think there's more to this story than he's telling us. But I'll offer Toyin one little test, just to make sure."

"What?" James frowned. "I warned you about going behind my back."

Ava smiled in return. "If it works, you'll thank me."

Chapter Twenty

"I don't feel like taking you home yet," Jackson said, as he navigated his Porsche on the city streets. The dark sky made the evening feel closer to midnight than nine o'clock. "Do you mind?"

"No. Actually, I sort of come alive at night."

He grinned. "Me too."

"Why did you dress up like your brother?"

His smile disappeared. "Because that's who they want me to be."

"You're so lucky you haven't had to meet any of my family yet."

Jackson tapped his finger against the steering wheel. "Hmm."

"Where are we going?"

"Shopping."

"Shopping? I've done enough shopping for a lifetime."

He sent her a curious glance. "You can never do too much shopping."

She decided not to argue. "What are we shopping for?"

"Clothes. I want to dress you up."

"Why?"

"I'm bored. I like to shop."

Toyin stood in a private room surrounded by mirrors dressed in an embroidered mesh lace mermaid dress in gunmetal gray. Before that she'd tried on a gold colored off the shoulder silk tunic dress and champagne colored v-neck beaded gown.

"Do you like it?" Jackson asked while he watched her from a white chaise lounge.

"What's not to like?"

He stood and walked towards her. "How does it feel?"

"Great."

Jackson touched the fabric, his knuckles brushing her skin causing her to tremble, before he looked at the assistant. "Cotton voile?"

"Yes, sir."

He looked at Toyin. "How are you with velvet?"

"I've never worn velvet."

"That's about to change."

They left the store with three large shopping and garment bags and Toyin wearing a crushed red-violet velvet dress while Jackson bought and wore a suit to match. She knew they both looked outrageous when they walked into a late night specialty bakery with an assortment of gourmet cookies, but she liked the feeling.

They ordered soft, moist chocolate chip cookies. Toyin never thought such a simple treat could taste so good.

"If you like this," Jackson said. "I also know an ice cream shop we can go to next time."

Next time. There would be a next time. This wonderful feeling could continue. Until this moment she hadn't realized how much she enjoyed his company. Being with him… She had missed this feeling the past several months. She'd thought fighting to save TJ Studios had been the true reason for her depression, but she'd missed him.

When she was in Vegas all her senses felt more heightened. The smells, the taste of the food, the bright lights. All this time she'd given credit to the city, but not the man. She felt that same way now. With Jackson, everything felt like a brand new adventure. Her eyes seeing the world in a new way. She'd looked but never really seen before. What others may deem unimportant, like the feel of fabric against the skin; the dash of pepper added to a meal; the taste of semi-sweet chocolate in a cookie, he made almost epic. She felt alive, vibrant in his presence. She now knew he hadn't been teasing her when he had called her beautiful. She was beautiful because he saw her that way. And that was how he made her feel. She never felt awkward, she felt interesting, witty. He was a magician.

Then why hadn't any other woman seen it too? Why had he had such bad luck in the past?

In two days she'd be marrying him again.

She licked chocolate from her lip then looked at him, making a decision. "You don't have to take me home tonight."

His eyes darkened. "Are you sure?"

"Do you care?"

His slow smile told her all she needed to know.

Chapter Twenty-one

I t had been one long night of foreplay.

That's what Toyin realized as she lay naked in his arms.

Every move, gesture or glance since the seemingly simple kiss in the hallway had been a careful, calculated seduction. From how he dressed her in silk and velvet, touching the fabric while also touching her skin; to the soft, moist cookies, the semi-sweet chocolate dissolving on her tongue. She remembered being mesmerized watching him lick a stray crumb from his mouth, the bright pink tip of his tongue sweeping slowly over his full bottom lip; she bit her own lip as she noticed him suck smothered chocolate from his thumb.

It had all been a subtle, decadent invitation.

And now she was at the ball. She glanced up at the soft recess lighting in his bedroom, the fine cotton sheets against her back. She'd expected him to be a bold, flamboyant lover, but instead he was a masterful one. As his warm hard body covered hers he smelled like brown sugar and vanilla just like the cookie, reminding her of when she was a child and had discovered finger painting, the wild thrill of pressing her hands in the wet colorful mixtures and splaying them on paper.

He was her canvas now and she let her hands run free along the front of his chest, down his back and along the hard, swollen length of him.

Jackson rolled on a condom then turned off the lights.

Toyin gasped before she started to laugh.

Jackson paused halfway on top of her. "What?"

"You have glow-in-the-dark condoms?"

She could hear the smile in his voice. "You like it?"

Toyin stroked it with her forefinger. "It's like getting intimate with a light saber."

"You'll be the first."

"To get intimate with a—"

"No," Jackson said with a chuckle, covering her body with his, "you'll be the first I've used them with. I know I'm taking a risk."

Toyin closed her legs around him, wanting him even closer. "I'm glad you did. Next time I'll wear my silver wig and an outfit you might find interesting."

"What?"

"It will be a surprise," she said then neither needed to say much else. Passion and desire consuming them.

Why had she denied herself this pleasure for so long? Since the moment he'd fallen on his knees and asked her to marry him she'd been tempted. Tempted to lose all inhibitions and forget her worries, if only for a moment. The magician in him made Lance disappear from her thoughts; Shanna became a whisper; Mama Bisi's disapproval a vague notion.

She wasn't a loser. A failure. A disappointment. She was a free, powerful woman claiming her desire. She didn't care about his past, the many women before her. Her passion left no room for fear.

He was hers tonight, feeding a burning sweet hunger. He'd married her and no other. No matter how long this lasted, she'd enjoy the moment. She would prove Ava wrong. She would prove them all wrong. Nobody knew them really.

But tonight they knew each other.

Chapter Twenty-two

His bride.

Jackson watched his future walk towards him wearing an A-line wedding dress, the beaded sequins seeming to sparkling under the chapel lights as her ivory train softly flowed behind her. She looked beautiful. He knew the taste of her lips, the sexy swell of her hips, the liquid heat between her legs, but he wanted more. Much more. He wanted to remove every inch of that ivory organza lace with steady, slow hands. See her eyes darken with desire. Hear her breath catch as he entered her. Feel her tighten around him all over again.

Dominion. He wanted every inch of her to be his and no one else's. Las Vegas hadn't been a coincidence or a mistake, but part of a careful plan. She still hadn't made the connection. He'd give her more time. It may not make a difference if she did.

But this moment meant more than he'd expected it to. He looked at her and she flashed him a soft nervous grin, as if in apology for everything. But she had nothing to feel sorry for. If he had to marry anyone, even briefly, he was glad it was her. With her, his life made sense. She didn't demand, she didn't cajole. He felt safe.

No, it was deeper than that. He knew he'd been in danger of losing his heart since the first moment, when she listened to him in Vegas and didn't judge. She came to warn him about the online story spreading. She came to get him from the club when he asked her. She was there when he needed her most. As he stood in front of the crowd and took her hand in his, Jackson felt his heart sliding into a dangerous abyss that he couldn't stop.

He knew he was in trouble. He knew his friends would laugh, his brother wouldn't believe him. But none of that mattered. He was in love.

Was it normal for a bride to want to cry on her wedding day? Toyin watched the pastor's mouth move wanting the day to be over. The night she'd spent with Jackson had been amazing. Everything had felt true, but this was a spectacle. Her cousin beamed at her and giggled at the most inopportune times. Soon Jackson would slide a ring on her finger and repeat words he didn't mean. She felt like bursting into tears her heart heavy with regret. Poor Jackson. He deserved better than this showcase. She did too.

Her mother looked so proud, her father pleased and Mama Bisi...

She knew she would still have to pay for her deception. Her grandmother wouldn't let this slide.

Toyin briefly looked over at Ava, remembering the strange request she'd given her when they'd had a moment alone after dinner.

"I didn't mean to upset you," Ava had said as they sat in the great room, the men had gone to talk in the library.

"It's okay," Toyin said. Ava sounded sincere.

"So I hope you won't take what I have to say the wrong way."

"What?"

"I'll pay you five thousand dollars not to sleep with him for a month."

"What?"

Ava held out a piece of paper. "It's for your own good and his."

Toyin stared at the contract stunned. What was it with this family and contracts? "What if we've already been intimate?"

Ava folded her arms.

"You don't think we have?" Toyin guessed.

"No, I don't."

"And you don't think our relationship is real?"

"Correct."

Toyin felt her heart hammering in her ears. Ava was clever and savvy. She didn't want to ruin this for Jackson. He said his job depended on Ava believing their relationship was real. "You're right. Jackson isn't interested in me that way, but I'm hoping—"

"I'll pay you to stop hoping. He's not worth it."

Toyin paused surprised by her words. "I thought you liked him."

"I do."

"And I love him."

Ava flashed a tight grin. "Let's see how much."

Toyin had signed the contract knowing she wouldn't comply. It was one of the reasons she'd slept with Jackson that same night.

Ava's presumption and challenge didn't sit well with her. The dare in her eyes had galled her. She didn't like that Ava thought she was using him. Ava should have better faith in him. He may come off showy and a little shallow, but there was much more to Jackson. He was more than just style, he also had substance and that's what made him memorable.

And why would sleeping with him be so terrible? What business was it of hers? Did Ava fear she'd try to get pregnant or something?

Considering the women he'd been with in the past she could understand Ava's concern, but it still didn't feel right.

That didn't stop her from trying to see it from another woman's perspective. Jackson had been drunk in Vegas, sober he'd never look at someone like her. If her sister and his brother hadn't come into the picture they would have gotten a quick annulment and she'd never see him again. They did make a strange pair. Who in their right mind could believe it was real? It was as likely as a stallion falling in love with a pug.

There were few men like her father who'd taken one look at her mother and said that she was the only one for him. That kind of fairy tale was not in the cards for her. This was purely business.

And common sense would keep her from even once imagining that any of this could be real. No matter how much she might wish it to.

Toyin turned sharply when she heard something move behind her. She saw Mama Bisi standing tall, her finger pointing at her in accusation.

"Stop the wedding! This marriage is doomed!"

Chapter Twenty-three

The crowd gasped and a wave of uneasy murmurs swept through the chapel.

"Mummy please," Toyin's mother said.

"Why is that woman shouting?" Rudy asked his brother James.

"I will not keep quiet," Mama Bisi declared. She motioned towards the two couples. "There is only one pair that should be at that altar." She pointed to Toyin again. "This must not continue. Walk away now before this farce becomes real." She narrowed her eyes. "I was right about Lance."

Toyin's cheek burned in remembrance.

"I am right about this. I am always right."

"I'm sorry," Toyin stuttered feeling weighted by the crowd's gaze on her. "I know I didn't consult with you first, but I care—"

"Don't lie so blatantly in a church. I know what I know and I see what I see. She doesn't deserve him."

Jackson frowned. "Madam—"

Mama Bisi rested a hand over her heart. "I love my granddaughter, she is my flesh, but I also know a poor match when I see one. Especially for you. I will not sit here and be silent."

Aunt Gretchen stood to her feet and pressed her hands together, pleading. "Mummy, please it's already done. This man is Toyin's choice and—"

Mama Bisi folded her arms and pinned Jackson with a stare. "His heart is too big." She shifted her gaze to Toyin. "Her heart is too small. They do not suit each other. There is no balance here. How can grass grow in a desert? Heed my words. Continue at your peril. You won't—"

Edgar stood. "He will do what he damn well wants to!"

The crowd turned to him.

"I do not know you," he said. "But I know Jackson. He is a Fortune and we Fortune men know our own minds. If my stepson wants to marry your granddaughter a hundred times he will do so. She's one of us now. Do not interfere."

Mama Bisi sent him an ugly look. "You use people as pawns. You have no idea what I'm saying."

"You can—"

"Enough!" Jackson said in a voice that left everyone quiet. He turned back to the pastor and said in a soft voice, "Continue."

The pastor hesitated then did so as the sound of Mama Bisi's heels pounded the ground as she stormed out of the church.

Toyin began to look back, but Jackson grabbed her hand, stopping her.

The rest of the wedding ceremony continued under a more somber air, but they both made it through. Tansy sniffed instead of giggled and before they parted she gave Toyin a watery kiss on the cheek.

In the limo on the way to the reception, Toyin held her head in her hands.

"She's wrong," Jackson said in a fierce tone. "I deserve you. I want you and no one else."

"She should have punished *me*, not you. I should have just left. Now everyone knows."

"They don't know anything."

"They'll suspect this isn't real. Now they'll—"

"I don't care."

Toyin lifted her head. "Yes, you do. She's right. I don't deserve you and now everybody knows it. How humiliating."

"She's wrong."

"She's never wrong."

Jackson's tone hardened. "She's wrong about us."

"Is she? What are we doing and who are we doing it for? For money and a job position? Does that even make sense? She probably won't speak to me again."

Toyin could understand her grandmother's words. Jackson was just a man who loved being in love. He could fall in love with anyone and be happy. However, she had never been in love. She liked people. Cared. But love…she'd never felt that way or maybe she'd never tried. Whatever the reason they were two very different people and that wasn't going to change.

"Is there a way to change your grandmother's mind?"

"Why would we want to do that? She knows this isn't real. It's all make believe."

"Is there a way?" he insisted.

"You're not making sense."

"Answer the question."

"I suppose nothing is set in stone. But I'd have to ask my mum—"

"Ask her."

"You don't see how lucky we are. We dodged a bullet. We can shorten this farce and—"

"I need this to work. Even if it's just for a year. I need the world to see that someone's willing to marry me because she wants me. Not because of a business deal or some other reason, just me."

"Jackson—"

"These last few days have been the best I've had in a long time. And it's because of you. I'm not asking you to love me for real. I didn't realize how much I needed this wedding until now."

"You heard my grandmother. I don't deserve you." She shook her head. "And stop saying she's wrong. She rarely is. I don't want to hurt you." Toyin called out to the driver. "Stop the limo."

"No," Jackson countered. He took her hands in his. "I know you're nervous about the reception. I know this has been a lot to take, but you're doing great. Don't worry."

"That doesn't help."

"What?"

She pulled her hands away. "Telling a person who's worried not to worry. It doesn't help."

"Okay, then relax. Take deep breaths. You don't have to do anything but smile."

"I'm not looking forward to an encore of humiliation. I was crazy to do this. I should have known Mama Bisi would make me pay." She hung her head. "I'll do everything else, please don't make me do this."

"I need you to. It's important that Ava and Edgar—"

"I wish I could." She held his gaze, pain squeezing her heart. "When we're alone it's like magic. I feel completely myself. It's wonderful but when others see us together something in me just…dies. And now Mama Bisi's words keep echoing in my head. I can't face another crowd. Tell them I'm sick. Tell them an emergency came up."

He grabbed her shoulders, desperate to convince her. "Everyone will be waiting for us."

"I can't go." Her voice cracked in misery. "I can't…I can't." Her mind raced but she couldn't find the words. She hated disappointing everyone. Why did she always have to be a disappointment?

Toyin rubbed her hands feeling as if she were being torn apart inside. She wasn't good with words. She wasn't good with people. She pulled out her cell phone and began to draw the image of a woman underneath an anvil about to fall. She showed it to him.

"I won't let that happen to you," Jackson said.

She drew another sketch showing the same woman and people pointing and laughing.

"I won't let that happen either."

She felt his chin as he rested it on her shoulder. It had a calming effect on her. She drew a woman melting into the floor.

"Not that either," he said in a quiet voice. He pointed to the screen. "Now draw me."

She looked at him in question.

"What?"

"The way you said that reminded me of—"

His gaze held hers, intense. "Who?"

She shook her head. "Just a boy I once knew. It was a long time ago."

"I acted like him?"

"It's was just a memory and you're not him so it doesn't matter."

"Are you sure?"

"That it doesn't matter?"

"No, that I'm not him."

She frowned. It was a strange question. "Of course you're not him. He had a different last name and—"

Jackson nudged her with his elbow. "Go on and draw me."

She began to sketch him in his tux.

"Now add a sword. Go on," he urged when she sent him a skeptical look.

She rolled her eyes. "Do you want a cape too?"

"Next time. Better yet, draw me with my shirt off."

"No."

"Naked?"

"No."

"I'll pose if that helps."

The memory of Jacky came back to her again. *Draw me. Draw me. I'm strong.*

She remembered standing outside of school and seeing Jacky show the picture she'd drawn for him to his mother and brother.

His brother…

His *twin* brother.

Jacky had a twin brother.

But that was impossible.

She remembered he was sad towards the end of the year. She heard from another student that he had to move. She remembered giving him another drawing and her address but he never wrote back. She always imagined him having three more girlfriends at whatever new school he would go to. She didn't cry like the others, but she did miss him. She wondered what he would be like now.

"Figured it out yet?" Jackson said.

She turned to him. "How can you be Jacky Brownson?"

He nodded and grinned. "In the flesh."

"I don't understand. Your name—"

"When my mother remarried my stepfather adopted us and gave us his surname. I started to go by 'Jackson' in the fourth grade."

"I don't know what to say."

"How about 'Long time no see'?"

"When did you know who I was?"

"The moment I heard someone say your name then I saw you in the New Worlds store. I was so shocked I toppled the display."

"Oh, right…that was you. I thought I remembered Ava…" She paused. "And now that I come to think of it—"

"Don't think of it," Jackson said with a groan. "It wasn't a good day.

"Why didn't you say anything before?"

"Pride, I was hoping that you'd finally recognize me. But then I got tired of waiting."

"You look…"

He lifted his chin in a haughty manner. "Amazing I know."

She rolled her eyes. "I should have known it was you. It was the lack of three girlfriends that threw me off. But then again you did have Ava, Enomwoyi and Sylvia." She shook her head. "I was so silly. I even gave you my address to write me so that we could be friends."

"I know."

"You never wrote me."

He nodded. "I know. Don't ask why. I was six. But I did make up for it." All humor left his voice and eyes. His gaze darkened and his voice deepened. "Toyin, I love you."

She smiled, sad. "You love sex."

"No, I *like* sex. Actually I like sex a lot but I *love* you."

She didn't know how to respond. Why was he saying this to her? Had he really married her on purpose because of some faint connection years ago? That didn't make any sense.

Finding out who he really was had come too late to save her. She shouldn't have fallen for him. Despite all his female woes he would keep having them. She now knew why he always got his heart broken. Her grandmother was right, his heart *was* too big. He was a man who loved being in love. The woman didn't matter, only the feeling. He was a man who could find pleasure anywhere. Once she was out of his life, he'd fall in love with someone else all over again.

Women would always be part of his life just as he'd been surrounded by girls as a child, as an adult it hadn't changed. There would be adoring women outside a club, in a bar, at the office. Everywhere.

And she'd fallen in love with him. But she would not continue down the doomed path Mama Bisi had predicted. Her tiny heart could not weather the pain he could inflict.

Toyin looked up at the driver. "Stop the limo."

"Toyin."

"I'm not going. I've already ruined my poor cousin's wedding day I won't ruin her reception as well. Don't worry, I'll fulfill my contract."

Jackson looked at her both hurt and surprised. "Contract? Did you hear what I said? I love you. I want to be with you. I want to spend my life with you."

When the limo pulled up to the curve, Toyin reached for the door. "Tell everyone I'm sorry."

He stopped her, his tone pleading. "Stay with me. I'll do whatever it takes to make you happy. I don't care if you don't love me."

Toyin looked at him for a long moment, her heart breaking. She opened the door and got out afraid she might stay, the cool autumn air chilling her skin spite the bright sunshine. She turned to him, blinking back tears. "That's the problem, Jackson. You should."

Chapter Twenty-four

"Sorry about your wedding," Ava said, entering Jackson's office at BioMed Solutions that Monday.

"Are you?" he said, doubtful.

"It was interesting. Has Toyin recovered?"

He hadn't seen her since she left the limo. But Ava didn't need to know that. He'd arrived at the reception alone and made excuses that everyone understood. But he hadn't been able to fool his brother James for long. While people were dancing he called him aside and said, "What's going on?"

"I told her who I really am," Jackson said, staring down at the champagne glass in his hand.

"That doesn't make sense."

He took a sip. "I mean who I was."

"And who were you?"

He lifted his gaze. "Jacky Brownson."

James looked at him sharply. "She knew you from before? Who is she?"

"A girl I knew from elementary school. The one I told you about. She drew me on the elephant."

James's brows shot up. "The girl who barely spoke? The girl who had you drawing hearts for days?"

"Shut up."

James looked at him for a long moment. "You fell in love with her, didn't you?"

Jackson looked down at his drink. "I didn't plan to. At first I only wanted to…" He let his words fall away.

James patted his brother on the back. "Once the shock wears off, I'm sure she'll understand."

But Jackson knew there was more to the story than his brother could fathom. He'd told her he loved her and she'd run away. How come his love was never enough?

He looked up at Ava now, dressed in her classic dark suit, in no mood for sarcasm or pity. "What do you want?"

"I want to talk to you and there's no point in saying no." She closed the door before she took a seat.

He reluctantly sat back in his chair and waited.

"Her grandmother's words hit a nerve and made me wonder. How long are you going to keep this up?"

"I'll keep it up for as long as it takes."

"What takes?"

He shrugged and came from behind his desk. "What do you want?"

Ava crossed her legs and sighed. "I'm sorry about thinking of suspending you. I was out of line."

Jackson folded his arms, wishing she'd get to the point. He glanced out his window at the clear blue autumn sky. "Is it summer already?"

"Alright, I'll get to the point. I don't like coincidences. I have a devious mind."

Jackson sat down beside her and rested his chin in his hand, bored.

"Toyin surprised me. By some stroke of luck you found someone who genuinely cares for you."

He slowly blinked. "Miracles do happen."

"Since I no longer thought that Toyin sought you out to use you in some way, I started to think about something else. You."

He straightened. "Me? I'm flattered."

"Don't be. What were you doing in Vegas? How did you happen to bump into someone whose comic store you've visited before? I find that very odd. You targeted her for a reason and it's not the reason everyone thinks, is it? I wonder what Toyin would say if I told her my suspicions?"

Jackson lightly rested his hand around her throat. "There are times when the thought of squeezing your neck is so tempting."

Ava grinned. "I'm right, aren't I? Who is she to you?"

"None of your business."

"Try again."

He tightened his hold a fraction, his gaze darkening. "So tempting."

"I like a little pain. Be careful or you'll make your brother jealous."

"What?"

She pushed his hand away. "Never mind. Now con-
fess."

"No."

"I will find out."

"Maybe."

Ava swung her foot. "Should I tell her that you're her
new landlord?"

Jackson swore. "How did you find out about that?"

Ava clicked her tongue. "Because I know you too well. I
remember how you reacted when we first entered New
Worlds. I also went to the store and heard about their
current plight with the landlord and then miraculously the
landlord said that all was well. That got me thinking. So I
tracked down said landlord and he was very cagey at first,
until I treated him to a drink or two, then he because a little
more chatty."

"What do you want?"

"I just told you."

"Toyin has nothing to do with you or this company. I'm
good at my job."

"I know that—"

"But you still want me out of the company."

"No," Ava said shocked. "I never said that."

"You wanted me suspended."

"For your own good."

"I know you love my brother, but don't pretend that
you ever loved me."

"I thought you'd forgiven me for that."

"I did too, until you went behind my back and tried to turn my family against me. This is all I have. I don't mind sharing, but I won't have it taken away."

"I wasn't trying to do that. Okay, I should have talked to you first, but I was worried about you. We all were. Really. I—" Ava suddenly stopped and swore. She jumped to her feet and stared at him reluctantly impressed. "You clever bastard. You put me on the defensive so you could distract me. That maneuver almost worked."

Jackson leaned back and held out his hands in surrender, a sly grin dancing on his lips. "A man can try."

"Actually, I may be helping you."

"How?"

"We both know you're terrible at judging women so the same night she came to dinner I had Toyin sign a contract—"

Jackson surged out his chair. "You did what!"

Ava calmly continued despite his outrage, "—to prove how much she loves you. I offered her five thousand dollars not to sleep with you for a month."

"What?!"

"If she holds out then the money is hers."

Jackson stared at her in shock.

"I know it sounds crazy, but it's for your own good. Money or you. It will be easy to see what she decides. She signed it right away." Ava paused, watching his expression change. "I can tell by that look that I did something right." She turned to the door. "You can thank me later."

Jackson heard the door close, but didn't move. She had given up five thousand dollars?

Toyin's words came rushing back to him. *That's the problem, Jackson. You should…* She was right, her loving him should matter. It should be what he wanted. What he craved. What he treasured. Claiming her heart should be as big a victory as convincing her to stay by his side. He'd been selfish. He'd only thought about how she made him feel, how much he wanted her. What he could do for her. He'd even made love a game, paying her to say the words. But just as he'd been blinded by data in the past, he'd been blinded by his own ego now.

Mama Bisi was right, I don't deserve you. There had been tears in her voice when she'd said that but he hadn't heard her pain. True pain. Her silent question. If I loved you back, would you even care?

He had to find her and tell her the answer was "I do."

Chapter Twenty-five

Toyin sat in the back office of New Worlds and stared down at her unfinished comic. She knew she would never finish it now. Every time she started, she thought of Jackson and it hurt too much.

She would not cry.

She would not regret loving him. She'd get over her feelings one day. Right now she had to focus on working with her lawyers to fight Shanna, try to save TJ Studios by drumming up new projects and clients and continue to run New Worlds. If pretending to be Jackson Fortune's wife helped her, she would treat it as the job it was and fulfill her contract. As part of their agreement, she was supposed to move to his place, but she didn't have the heart yet. Perhaps next week. Perhaps next month. She had to think about the money.

Her lawyers had overwhelmed Shanna's enough that they were thinking of settling. The money from the Fortunes was worth it. After a few months she'd never have to see Jackson again and he'd shower someone else with his affection.

Toyin looked up at the framed photos on her walls. She hadn't expected her world to feel grey without him. She'd expected to leave the limo feeling liberated. She'd walked away. She'd had the courage to admit she was wrong. She would let Mama Bisi choose her next match. She didn't care if she loved him or not. Love was for losers. She no longer wanted to be that.

Toyin tasted her tears before she felt them.

Jackson never made her feel like a loser. Even as a child when Mrs. Lorquette made her feel stupid, he made her feel smart. When Lance made her feel discarded, Jackson made her feel wanted. When her family made her feel like a disappointment, Jackson made her feel like a success.

Something clicked in her brain. She loved him. And that love didn't make her feel low or worthless. It didn't make her feel like a loser. It made her feel strong and alive.

And angry.

Toyin pushed the comic aside and grabbed her keys.

Nearly an hour later Toyin faced Mama Bisi in the living room of her parents' house. A Fela Kuti protest song played softly in the background, while the smell of baked plantain scented the air.

"You were missed at the reception," her father said. He sat on the sofa next to her mother. He cast a nervous glance at Mama Bisi before returning his gaze to Toyin's angry features.

"We managed a nice chat with Jackson," her mother said, trying to fill the silence.

"Seems a nice chap."

"Very nice. He—"

"I came to speak to Mama Bisi," Toyin said in a low voice. "In private, if I may."

Her parents nodded then left the room.

Mama Bisi folded her hands in her lap and fixed her with a cool look. "What do you have to say to me?"

Tears gathered in her eyes, but she felt no shame in them. "You say you are never wrong. But you were wrong Saturday. My heart isn't small. My love isn't worthless. It's as deep and true as anyone's. And I am able to love many things. My heart is big enough to hold them all—my family, my friends, my art, my business and…and yes a man. A man you don't think deserves me." She took a steadying breath. "But he does, because I can love him like no one else can. He may not see it. He may not care, because it's not flashy and showy like his. I may not express myself the way he does or the way others think I should, but I still have a heart." She pounded her chest. "A big heart that beats and bleeds and longs and dreams and loves just like any other heart does."

Toyin briefly covered her eyes, her voice shaking. "It wasn't fair what you did to me on my wedding day." She wiped her tears and met her grandmother's gaze. "No matter how right you felt you are, you hurt me, wounded me to the core because you shamed me in front of the man I love."

Mama Bisi lifted her chin. "And does he know this?"

Toyin wiped away a tear confused. "What?"

"Does this man you tell me you love, know that you love him?"

"I…no but—"

"You don't think it matters. You don't have the courage to make it matter."

Toyin frowned. "I don't understand."

A tiny smile touched her lips. "I lied. The moment I met him I knew."

"You met him?"

She nodded, but didn't explain how. "I could not scare him away. I knew he was a good match for you, but I knew that I could never convince that rebellious heart of yours to accept him. You would be contrary just for the sake of it. I pushed you on your special day so that you could see what was staring you in the face. What you thought was false has always been real."

"But how did you—?"

"Your sister explained the true facts to me. That she forced you to reveal your secret marriage. Don't blame her; you know I have my ways."

Toyin stared at her stunned. "Are you saying that Jackson and I are meant to be?"

Mama Bisi nodded. "Yes. On your own you managed to find the right man to love who will love you back."

Toyin thanked her grandmother then left her parents' house in a daze. Mama Bisi approved? She saw Jackson and her together?

She didn't know what to do. Should she call him? Go by his place? No, she couldn't risk that. What if he was with someone else? She loved him but what if he didn't care?

Toyin drove home.

She found Jackson outside her apartment door. Before she could ask him what he was doing there, he held out a booklet.

"I did a 24-hour comic I want you to read," he said.

Her hands trembled but she took it from him and unlocked the door. She nervously dropped the keys on the floor and quickly picked them up not knowing how to feel. She felt thrilled that he'd come to see her, but also fearful that she'd broken whatever bond they'd had. She'd never felt this awkward with him before.

"Do you want something to drink?"

Jackson looked around her apartment briefly smiling at the picture of Storm. "No."

Toyin sat down and looked at the stick figure drawings he'd given her. She pointed. "What is this supposed to be?"

Jackson sat down beside her. Close enough to touch. "It's a man on a horse."

She swallowed, aware of his nearness. He smelled like mint. "It looks like a twig."

"I'll narrate it for you. Just listen." He motioned to the first page. "It starts on this panel."

"Okay."

He tapped the stick figure. "It's a story about this man."

"Does the man have a name?"

"No, he's just a man who likes to be a hero. We'll call him The Hero. Because of this trait he always falls for women who trick him."

"Is this why he's standing next to a heart with an arrow in it?"

"Yes. Now be quiet." Jackson pointed to another panel. "One day The Hero sees someone from his past, someone who he'd rescued before. A girl who scared him a little."

"Scared him?"

"Yes, don't interrupt. She scared him because she was different. She barely spoke, but he knew she was smart. Smarter than he was. So when he saw her again he wanted to rescue her once more. He would come by the market and spy on her and learn more about her and wondered what he could do because she didn't seem to need anything. Until one day he heard something that finally gave him that chance.

"It was one of those moments of fate people talk about. Now This Woman that The Hero wanted to rescue was seeing someone else. Let's just call him 'The Bastard.' "

Toyin couldn't help a giggle. "I could call him something else."

"So could I, but this is my story and I want to keep it clean. Anyway, The Hero went to the bank one day and overheard The Bastard talking to a woman we'll call…hmm…The Bitch."

Toyin started to laugh.

Jackson continued. "The Hero heard The Bastard talking to The Bitch about a conference in Las Vegas and how he planned to propose to This Woman and how they could cover their misdeeds. So—"

"Wait, you can't keep calling her 'This Woman'."

"Yes, I can."

"Call her 'The Heroine'."

He shook his head. "No, it's my story."

"Please."

He sighed. "The Hero knew…The Heroine—"

"Thank you."

"—would need his help so he flew to Nevada to find a way to stop her, but he caught her finding out the truth on her own. So—"

"So he followed her to the hotel bar."

He turned a page. "You're interrupting."

"Sorry."

"He stayed away wondering what he should do. Then he gathered the courage to approach her at the bar."

"Don't you think The Heroine would have preferred that The Hero told her what he knew before she left for Vegas?"

"Would she have believed him?"

Toyin paused. "Probably not."

"Any more questions?"

"No. Go on."

"The Hero persuaded This Woman—excuse me—The *Heroine* to marry him because he thought it would be fun and it would make her happy. And he felt he had won when she needed money, which he had plenty of and he convinced her to stay by his side. The Hero didn't expect to fall in love with The Heroine, but he did. Then he got cocky. Because he forgot one thing. He hadn't won the true prize."

"This is a very long story."

"Do you want me to finish?"

She bit her lip and nodded.

"He hadn't won her heart. So he took his sword and killed himself."

Toyin looked with dismay at the last panel of the stick figure with a sword through his chest, bleeding. She looked up at him outraged. "That's an awful story."

Jackson's eyes searched hers, his voice thick and unsteady. "How would you end it?"

She chose her words carefully. "The Hero would find out how much The Heroine loved him and he would realize that he didn't have to do anything to be loved."

His eyes brightened with joy then darkened with passion. "I like your ending better," he said, gathering her in his arms.

"Me too." She wrapped her arms around his neck, her fears wiped away in the glow of love. "Mama Bisi told me we're a perfect match."

Jackson pressed his lips against hers then whispered, "I always knew that."

"Think we should get married?" she teased him.

Jackson laughed. He held her tighter, letting her know he had no plans to ever let her go. "No, I think we deserve a honeymoon."

Toyin nodded, seeing their lives bound together forever. "Me too."

In case you missed it...

Turn the page for a taste of *A Tempting Proposal*, Book 1 in The Fortune Brothers.

Chapter One

A wife.

He was not supposed to end up with a wife. At least not yet. He had plans, dreams and goals. This was not one of them. James Fortune gritted his teeth as he listened to the melodious soft voice of Pastor Valentine, her pink reading glasses hanging precariously low on her nose, inches away from falling. Much like the present state of his life.

He'd managed to achieve most of his goals. He'd gotten degrees in both Biology and Mechanical Engineering and become head of Research and Development at BioMed Solutions. Yes, it was his stepfather's company, and at thirty-four he was the youngest division manager in the company, but no one could deny that under James's watch and careful leadership more innovative projects had been developed and funded. Morale was up and the people liked him, unlike his predecessor, a charismatic man who wasted money on pet projects that only highlighted his interests instead of others or furthering the success of the company.

James knew he wouldn't stay in management for long, he wanted to launch his own ventures, but he'd given himself two more years before he would embark on his next career goal. He believed in taking calculated risks.

Not insane ones.

James glanced at Pastor Valentine's reading glasses again, noticing that they'd fallen down a little further. He flexed his fingers resisting the urge to say something. Couldn't she feel them moving? Would she let them fall off her face?

He inwardly groaned, knowing his attention and annoyance were misplaced. It wasn't the pastor's glasses that really bothered him, or even the sound of her voice, which always reminded him of someone in a musical about to burst into song (he half expected her to snap the bible shut, rip off her glasses and start singing), it was the entire ceremony.

He knew that what he was doing was not only reckless and insane, but criminal. He'd never done anything illegal in his life. Okay, so maybe he had done some speeding, and once—just once—when he was under charged for an item at the grocery store, he didn't report it. But he was a law abiding citizen. A good man. Now he was a fraud. He'd put his reputation and future on the line all because of Jackson.

His twin brother was supposed to be standing at the altar, inside this elegant stone cathedral, bearing the scrutiny of hundreds of guests from the Americas and the Caribbean, marrying the beautiful, brilliant and influential Ava Simone Hughes.

James made sure to keep his gaze on the pastor, instead of her. He knew Ava's brilliance by her reputation. She'd won an international science prize at sixteen and her research in the field of biodegradable implants preceded her. Her findings were almost legendary in the industry; her influence was also unavoidable from her innovative lab work to her connection with top universities. But her beauty.

That was his weak point.

He feared his heart would stop when the cathedral's double doors opened and she walked down the red carpeted, flower adorned aisle towards him. Damn, why did it have to be *him*? He'd always found her attractive, even in the dark suits she liked to wear—sometimes with trousers other times with a skirt, always black or dark blue—but at this moment she was breathtaking in a floor-length tulle lace gown with beaded sequins. The ivory colored fabric, accented with a translucent hint of sky blue, complimented her exquisite dark skin.

She looked like a princess, her carriage regal, her fine high cheekbones striking, but he knew she was no innocent, blushing bride. She had dangerous brown eyes and without the benefit of a veil to shield him from her gaze, he had to face them head on and make sure she didn't suspect a thing. She was the kind of woman who could kiss a man tenderly on the lips and drive a steak knife through his heart at the same time. He knew his deception would come at a price if she ever found out.

He couldn't let that happen. He had to be careful.

He'd discovered that the first time Jackson formerly introduced her to him. Her keen, steely gaze hit him like a brick. With one look he'd seen her power and vulnerability and that combination had floored him. He knew a woman like her could be trouble, but his brother liked courting trouble so James had dismissed the feeling. He couldn't dismiss it now.

James briefly looked at the ceiling. He was doing the right thing. Jilting a woman like Ava would have far reaching consequences and too much was at stake. He was doing this because his brother was too weak to accept his duty to his family and the business.

James took a deep breath, wishing he would wake up from this nightmare, but when he touched Ava's hand and slid a white gold band of hand selected diamonds on one of her long, slender fingers he knew it was all too real.

At least his hands didn't tremble and he didn't drop the ring as he feared, trying his best to ignore the reality that every action he made was being watched. Unlike his brother who welcomed it like a parched horse at a watering hole, he didn't like being in the spotlight. James inwardly groaned. He could use a drink right now. Something cold and biting. He stood stock still as he felt a trail of sweat slide down his back. He remembered saying "With this ring…" but the rest was a blur as he fought to imitate his brother's casual flair in every word and gesture.

He'd never switched places with Jackson before, despite all his brother's urgings when they were younger, trying to convince him that it would be fun. James never thought it would be either fun or practical. Definitely not practical. Even as a child he knew a day in the life of his brother would be exhausting.

Instead of being alone in the library, with his science club, discussing a new discovery with a teacher or training with the track team, he'd be charming the students (especially the girls, but guys liked him too) and teachers of both genders, and partying. There would be too many names to remember, too many places to be. He liked to live a regimented, quiet life and said he'd never switch places. Ever.

He'd been wrong.

But he didn't have a choice.

About the Author

Dara Girard is an award-winning, national bestselling author of more than forty books including *Sweet Temptation*, *Midnight Promise, Unexpected Pleasure, Just One Look* and *The Amber Stone*. Dara loves to travel and hear from readers.

You can write her at:
contactdara@daragirard.com
or
P.O. Box 10345
Silver Spring, MD 20914

If you'd like to receive a reply, please send a self-addressed stamped envelope. Visit daragirard.com to join her newsletter and be the first to find out about current and upcoming releases.

www.ingramcontent.com/pod-product-compliance
Lightning Source LLC
Chambersburg PA
CBHW060600190726
48283CB00003B/1090